MURDERED BY WINE

A Cedar Bay Cozy Mystery - Book 13

BY

DIANNE HARMAN

Published by: Dianne Harman
www.dianneharman.com

Interior, cover design and website by
Vivek Rajan

ISBN: 978-1976037665

CONTENTS

Acknowledgments

ACKNOWLEDGMENTS

I'm always asked how I come up with ideas for my books. Even I have to admit this one came out of left field. Our daughter-in-law is a wine scholar. She's received almost every certificate one can acquire for American and French wines, and she also teaches the subject. My husband and I recently met her and our son in Sonoma, California, and naturally, we had to do some wine tasting.

While touring a boutique winery our guide showed us the wine vat barn. The guide mentioned that the winemakers had to be very careful when they worked around a wine fermentation vat, because occasionally a winemaker could become overcome by the carbon dioxide gas given off by the fermenting wine, fall in a wine vat, and die. Needless to say, I immediately went on alert and knew this could become the subject of a new book! And so it did.

I want to thank all of the wonderful people in Sonoma who hosted us and allowed us to enjoy their restaurants, their wineries, and shared their beautiful city with us. We so appreciate your gracious hospitality. Thanks!

To Vivek and Tom: My undying appreciation for all you do. I've thanked you many times before, so I won't bore the readers with a laundry list of all the things each of you does to help make my books bestsellers. You know how much I value what you do for me.

And to my readers: Thank you for continuing to buy and borrow my books. Because of you, I'm fortunate to always be on a number of bestseller lists, not the least of which was being a USA Today Bestselling Author on July 6, 2017. Thank you for making all of this happen!

Win FREE Paperbacks every week!

Go to www.dianneharman.com/freepaperback.html and get your FREE copies of Dianne's books and favorite recipes immediately by signing up for her newsletter.

Once you've signed up for her newsletter you're eligible to win three paperbacks. One lucky winner is picked every week. Hurry before the offer ends!

CHAPTER ONE

Angela Lucci opened the kitchen door of her home that overlooked the Moretti vineyard just north of Sonoma, California, and inhaled the fresh smell of grapes that was still in the air from the recent harvest. Her long raven hair tumbled over her shoulder, grazing the flawless tanned skin of her uncovered arms. It was a clear fall day, and she welcomed the fresh breeze that met her on the porch. She knew the wine that was fermenting in the large stainless steel vats was doing fine. The crush, or the harvest of the grapes, had gone well. As usual, Juan, the man in charge of hiring the seasonal help required to handpick the grapes, had chosen his workers wisely.

She turned back to where her husband, Matteo, was standing, enjoying the last few sips from his morning coffee, and said, "I didn't think I'd like it when we came to California and had to leave our families in Italy, but I'm glad we did."

Matteo's mustache moved as he smiled at his wife. Setting his cup of coffee on the counter, he pulled her to him.

"Certainly, *Signor* and *Signora* Moretti have given us so much," Angela continued. "I mean, think about it, Matteo. We could never afford a large house like this on our own and live in one of the most beautiful places in all of California. I've gotten to really like the people here, both at the vineyard, and in town, and I love my job. When I was a young woman studying winemaking in Umbria, I never dreamed it would lead me here."

"Or to me?" Matteo murmured, kissing her forehead.

She smiled at him and continued, "Nor did I think I would find my future husband there. I'm glad my parents agreed to send me to the school in Umbria. And how fortunate both of us were to get jobs with the Moretti vineyard in Tuscany. I'm grateful that when *Signor* and *Signora* Moretti asked me to be their winemaker at their new vineyard in Sonoma they had a friend, *Signor* Romano, who also had a vineyard here in Sonoma, and that he would hire you as a winemaker. I think we have to be the luckiest two people in the world."

"So do I, *amore mio*," the muscular dark-haired man said, stroking his wife's hair. His large brown eyes and thick eyelashes were still capable of sending warm shivers throughout Angela's body "but I wish the wine *Signor* Romano produces at his vineyard was as coveted as the Moretti label. I envy you for being the head winemaker here."

Angela nuzzled closer to him. "Aah, Matteo, we've talked about this before, but I never think of us as having different jobs. We're a couple. I just happen to be working for *Signor* Moretti, and you just happen to be working for *Signor* Romano. I think our jobs are very much the same. We are equals."

"That's very gracious of you, Angela, but we both know that the wines from the Moretti Winery are far more highly regarded than the Romano wines," Matteo said with a sigh. "I do the best I can with what they have on the property, but every year in tasting competitions our wines always place second to those from the Moretti Winery."

"I wish it were otherwise," Angela said, staring into Matteo's eyes, "but for now let's just enjoy where we are. I think it's a good thing we both worked for *Signor* Moretti's parents at their vineyard in Tuscany. I'm sure if we just applied for the position and they didn't personally know us, we never would have been hired."

"Angela, it's not we, it's you. I didn't get the position, you did."

"Matteo, please, not again," Angela said soothingly. She hated it when Matteo's eyes clouded over. "Even if I do work for the Moretti Winery, and yes, my position as the winemaker at a prestigious winery is probably thought of as more desirable than yours by some people, but I don't consider it to be so, and that's all that's important. You are the head of our household and always will be."

Matteo pulled away from her with a jolt. "Don't speak to me in that condescending tone of voice. It sounds like you think I'm some sort of idiot. He slammed his fist on the counter and then stomped out the door with an angry bitter look on his face.

Angela's stare followed him. "Matteo, where are you going?" she asked in a frightened voice.

"To the Romano winery, the second-rate Romano winery, I might add," he said as he jumped in his truck and roared off down the road to the main highway in a cloud of dust.

Angela sighed, thinking his ego had gotten in the way of a lovely fall morning. She wished there was something she could do to convince him that his job was not secondary to hers, but no matter how hard she'd tried, it simply hadn't worked in the past. She looked at her watch and realized it was time to get the wine samples for Bob, the UPS delivery man, to take to the special lab in town that *Signor* Moretti used to test the quality of his wine production. He was very committed to making sure that each vat of wine was problem free and that required a daily analysis of the wine in each vat, whatever the season, whatever the weather.

CHAPTER TWO

"Here are the morning wine samples, Bob," Angela said, as she pulled up the zipper of her baggy sweatshirt. The morning air had cooled, and she could feel goosebumps on her arms. "The wine has a few more days until it will be ready to transfer to the barrels for aging. I'll check the vats again this evening, like I do every night, to make sure the wine is okay, but from what I've been seeing, we're almost there."

Bob Alty, who was there to collect the wine samples for the lab, regarded her with admiration. "Angela, I think you have the greatest job anyone could ever dream of having. I mean, how many people in the world can say that they're the brains and the palate behind the best wine made in Sonoma. And I didn't even mention that you get to taste the wines that you make for free. Considering how pricey those wines are, that's a pretty nice perk." He arranged the samples in a special carrying case made just for that purpose and snapped it shut.

"I know, Bob. Sometimes I have to pinch myself to see if this is real. I just wish my husband shared your point of view."

Bob raised his eyebrow and said, "Good grief, Angela, what could possibly be his problem? He's married to a gorgeous Italian woman..."

She laughed as she interrupted him, "Bob, I am hardly gorgeous.

Italy is full of women far prettier than I am."

"Hate to disagree with you, Angela, but with that Cleopatra hair, your flashing brown eyes, and a figure that even the jeans and sweatshirts you wear can't hide, I think your husband is a very lucky man." Bob gave Angela a pointed look as he waited for his words to sink in, "and I can add from what I've heard, that I'm not the only one in Sonoma who thinks that. Plus, he's the one responsible for the excellent wines the Romano winery makes."

"Thank you, Bob," Angela murmured, lowering her head, "but Matteo doesn't quite see it that way. He is Italian, very Italian, and in Italy the man is the most important person in the marriage. My being the winemaker at a winery that is more prestigious than his is very hard on his ego, but I don't know what to do about it. It worries me."

A concerned Bob bent his head down to meet Angela's eyes once more. "Hey, you don't need to do anything, Angela. He's a fool if he doesn't realize what he has. Don't lower your standards to accommodate his outdated macho thinking. That's nuts."

Angela gave him a grateful smile, but didn't respond.

"I'd love to talk longer, but I've got to get these samples to the lab and then run the rest of my route. See you tomorrow," he said as he walked out to his truck. If he'd known that would be the last time he would ever see Angela, he might have stayed a little longer and told her how seeing her every day was the highlight of his job. He'd regret to his dying day that he hadn't stayed.

*****

Later that morning, Angela greeted Caitlin Sanders, the young woman who was interning at the winery in the mornings. Part of the master's degree program she was enrolled in at the University of California at Davis, known world-wide for its wine studies program, was to have hands-on experience at a winery. Being the intern at the prestigious Moretti Winery was the culmination of Caitlin's education. After interning there, all she wanted when she graduated with her degree was to have the job Angela had. Quite simply, she wanted to be the winemaker at the Moretti Winery.

"Caitlin, we have a busy day ahead of us. The wine in the vats will probably be ready for transferring to the barrels within a few days. I want you to be with me this morning, so I can show you what we're looking for. We also need to go out to the vineyards and walk some of the rows with Juan. I haven't been out there since the crush, and one of the most important things you're going to have to do as a winemaker is make sure that everything is going well with the vines. Believe me, that's just as important as what's happening in the vats."

Caitlin nodded, and smiled eagerly.

Angela continued, "Good girl. I see you've got sandals on, so you're already wearing the type of shoes that most of us do."

"Yes. I noticed that the people who go out to the vineyards, and then back in the buildings, all wear them."

Angela looked at the young woman, thinking how very intelligent she was and wishing she could tell her not to be quite so vocal about how much she wanted to take Angela's place and be the winemaker at the Moretti Winery. Several people had mentioned to Angela that Caitlin had told them that because she had the best grades of anyone in the program at UC Davis, she was certain, with her master's degree, and her finely tuned taste buds, she would someday soon make wines that were even better than those presently being made at the Moretti Winery.

Aah, youth, Angela thought. *From what I've read, these millennials think they are the equals of everyone, and if they have a degree, experience really doesn't matter. Someday she will learn that experience matters as much as anything else in winemaking, maybe more, but from what I know of her, she wouldn't be able to understand what I mean. She'll simply have to learn it.*

When they returned from their walk in the vineyards, Caitlin prepared to leave. As she packed up her things, she turned to Angela and said, "By the way, Angela, I know you take a sample from the vats in the morning and send them to the lab in town, but as I recall, you once told me you also take a sample in the evenings. What do you do with those?"

"I take a small sip to make sure they are as I wish them to be. At seven at night, no matter what, I test them. It is very important that the samples be taken at the same time each morning and at the same time each evening."

"That makes sense. See you tomorrow," Caitlin said as she walked out to the parking lot located in front of the winery.

After Caitlin left, Angela went home for lunch, looking forward to seeing her fox terrier, Foxie, who could always barely contain herself when Angela came home. When she'd seen the adorable little puppy for sale at a vineyard down the road, she knew she had to have her.

Foxie and Angela had bonded from the moment she brought her home, and she'd been relentless in her training. As a result, Foxie was heel trained and even when they walked the rows of vines in the vineyard, she stayed next to Angela. Matteo had never been very thrilled with Foxie, and it was one of the stresses in their marriage, but the primary one was Angela being the head winemaker at the Moretti Winery.

When she arrived home, Foxie ran around in joyous circles, certain that treats and walks were to follow. Angela's face lit up. It was hard not to relax with Foxie around. "Okay, girl, I have a little time. Let's take a walk. You've been fenced in long enough." She took Foxie's leash off the hook on the kitchen wall and attached it to her collar as she put some dog cookies in her pocket.

Half an hour later, a very tired Foxie and her master returned to the house. Angela knew she had a lot of paperwork which needed to be done that afternoon. With all the frantic work involved during the time of the crush, she'd gotten behind, and when she'd gotten out of bed that morning she made a vow that nothing was going to interfere with her need to catch up on her paperwork. She bolted down a sandwich and drank a glass of iced tea, then hurried back to her office at the winery.

CHAPTER THREE

The afternoon went by quickly for Angela. Her office was located on the ground floor behind the vat room and twice she had to go up the steps leading to the first floor and to the vineyard manager's office for some paperwork she was missing.

The second time she walked down the hall to his office she noticed four people in the private tasting room maintained for tour guests. They were with the winery tour guide, Josie, who was explaining the differences between the wines that were being served. Angela had always thought if she was someone who just enjoyed having a glass of wine, coming to the Moretti Winery and going on a private tour would be an excellent way to learn about wine.

Josie, a bubbly blond, waved her into the room and introduced her as the Moretti Winery's winemaker. "The reason the Moretti wines are so well-known throughout the world is all due to this woman, Angela Lucci, our winemaker," Josie said, beaming. "If you enjoy the wines you're tasting, and who wouldn't, Angela is the one who decides exactly what grape and what blends of grapes go into each bottle of wine we produce. It's an incredibly difficult job, but no one does it better than Angela."

They applauded, and Angela smiled at them. "I hope you enjoy your visit with us, and of course, I hope you enjoy the wine. You're very fortunate to have Josie as your guide. There's none better in Napa or Sonoma. She's one of the few," she looked at Josie and said, "maybe the only one in our area who has received a diploma from the Wine and Spirits Education Trust. Right, Josie?"

A red-faced Josie grinned and said, "Yes, I was very fortunate."

Angela looked at the group and said, "I need to take care of some paperwork, but I assure you that you're in the hands of the best tour guide in the valley. Enjoy your afternoon." She waved to them as she walked down the hall to the office of Jim Barstow, the manager of the Moretti Winery.

"Hi, Jim," Angela said as she walked in through the open door of his office. "Guess I'm being quite the pest today, but I need one more file. It's the one on the tests from last week. *Signor* Moretti likes them daily and with the crush, I haven't had time to send them to him. He'll probably be over here tomorrow to see how the primary fermentation is doing, so I want to show him the test results and assure him that there aren't any problems."

Jim looked up from his desk which was strewn with paperwork, candy wrappers, and empty soda cans. Angela often wondered how Jim worked in all that mess, but he assured her there was a method to his desktop filing system. No one was allowed to remove anything from his desk, even the people who cleaned the offices.

"Angela, with you on top of things, I think the one thing *Signor* Moretti doesn't worry about is what's happening at the Moretti Winery. Too bad his wife doesn't feel the same way."

"What do you mean? Has she said something about me?" Angela asked as she stood up from the file cabinet where she'd been crouched down. "I've always had a feeling she didn't like me for some reason, but I don't know why," she said as she tucked a strand of hair behind her ear. "On the other hand, he seems very happy with my work."

"I don't think it has anything to do with your work," Jim said, adjusting his glasses. "I think it has to do with you. I've noticed she's uncomfortable any time there's another woman around who's attractive, and fortunately, or unfortunately, you fall into that category. It doesn't help that I've heard him tell his wife a number of times how lucky they are to have you. When a woman's concerned that her husband might look outside the marriage for enjoyment, that's the one thing she doesn't want to hear."

"Jim, that's ridiculous. You know that."

Jim leaned back, and his chair creaked. "That I do, but I don't think *Signora* Moretti is convinced. Believe me, Angela, it's nothing you've done. She just happens to be the owner of the biggest inferiority complex I've ever seen."

Angela shrugged. "Well, there's nothing I can do about it. That's her problem. I'm totally committed to Matteo," she said as she again bent over the file drawer. She didn't see Jim roll his eyes in a time-old gesture as he cast his eyes on her very desirable figure. "Okay, I found what I need." She straightened up, holding a buff-colored folder in her hands. "I'm almost finished for today. Time to go home, get a pot of minestrone going, check the wine vats one last time, and settle in for the night. See you tomorrow."

"Have a good evening, Angela. As hard as you work around here, you deserve it." Jim's gaze lingered on Angela's shapely form as she left the room.

CHAPTER FOUR

Angela walked into her house and was immediately greeted by Foxie, who was beside herself with joy. Like many dogs who seem to be afraid their owner will never return when the owner leaves the house, Foxie was thrilled when Angela returned from wherever she had gone. She danced around, jumped up and down, and ran circles around Angela, while at the same time she gleefully barked and yipped.

"Hey, you crazy little girl," Angela said, laughing, and happy with the warm welcome. She patted Foxie on the head and went into the kitchen to make a big pot of minestrone soup. The nights had turned cool in the valley and warm soup with a salad and bread which had been generously dusted with Italian herbs sounded perfect. Matteo wasn't home yet, but she wasn't surprised. He often stayed and had a glass of wine with *Signor* Romano when they were finished with work for the day.

After the soup and salad had been made, she hummed to herself as she set the table, putting fresh candles on the table, hoping that Matteo's mood was better than it had been when he'd left that morning. She glanced at her watch and realized it was time for her to take the evening samples from the wine vats.

Angela knew she was one of the few, if not the only, winemaker in the valley who tested each vat every evening by tasting a miniscule amount of the wine contained in it. When she'd first started working as the winemaker at the Moretti Winery, she did it to make sure the wine was progressing as it should be, with balanced acidity and sugar levels – and just the right amount of fruitiness. Now she thought it would be bad luck to discontinue the practice.

Angela turned to make sure that everything was in place for dinner in case Matteo came back while she was gone. He liked things a certain way, and she didn't want to do anything to anger him any further, after the argument they'd had that morning.

"Ready, Foxie? Time for our nightly walk over to the vat barn." Foxie may not have known many words, but walk was definitely one that propelled her small body into a state of ecstasy. Just the thought of another walk with her mistress was cause for running over to where her leash was kept, accompanied by a small joyful bark.

The two of them walked in the early evening darkness the short distance to the building where the vats were located. The vineyard was silent with the only sound being faint strains of music coming from one of the nearby residences. As usual, Angela secured Foxie's leash to a post before she unlocked the heavy double doors, closing them partially behind her after she entered. She knew tying Foxie up was probably unnecessary, since shedding dog hair had never been a problem with her, but even so, Angela wanted to make sure that no stray dog hairs landed in any of the wine vats during the brief time she opened the containment lids and took her nightly sips.

She walked up the steep flight of metal stairs attached to the outside of the twenty-foot-tall stainless-steel fermenting vat, leaned over the containment lid, slid it back, and peered down at the dark wine. She was just getting ready to dip the small wooden cup attached to a long metal handle which she'd brought with her into the wine in the vat when someone grabbed her from behind and held her face over the open fermenting wine vat. In less than thirty seconds, she was overcome by the carbon dioxide fumes generated by the fermentation process.

The person behind her pushed her unconscious body into the vat of wine, where she floated face down in the cauldron of bubbling fermenting wine. Angela never heard Foxie's frantic barking as she saw her mistress disappear into the tank and the murderer run down the stairs, open the heavy doors a little more, and slip outside. It was fortunate for Foxie that the murderer heard approaching voices, or she might have been the next one pushed into the wine vat.

CHAPTER FIVE

"Mike, I just got an email from Julia," Kelly said as she walked into the kitchen. "She and Brad want to meet us in Sonoma. You know, she's been teaching classes on wine at the college over in Calico Gold, and she's ready for a little R & R. She'd like to do some wine tasting over there. Sounds kind of fun. We've never done anything like that, although I think I better switch to water after my two-glass limit."

Mike looked up from his newspaper and raised an eyebrow. "Does that mean they won't be bringing Ella and Olivia? I don't think they'd enjoy a vacation like that."

"No, your cherished grandchildren will have to stay at home. Wine tasting rooms and children are not synonymous." Kelly reached for the coffee pot on the stove and started to fill the two mugs on the countertop.

When Mike had married Kelly, a widow with two grown children, he'd shortly inherited two step grandchildren as well. Her daughter, Julia, had married Brad, a widower with two daughters, and within a few months of their wedding Julia had adopted the two girls whose mother had died from a drug overdose.

Mike was a man who had lived by himself for many years following his divorce, but after his marriage to Kelly, he eagerly took to being a stepfather and particularly his new role of step-grandparent. He used every excuse he could to see the young girls, who adored him. When his elderly aunt was murdered and he inherited her large ranch in Calico Gold, he adopted Julia, so she could inherit it on his death rather than having it sold to a stranger. He often said it was the best thing he'd ever done.

Kelly set the mugs on the table and sat down beside Mike, who reached for the one Ella and Olivia had given him the previous Christmas, that said, "Trust Me – I'm a Sheriff." He lifted the cup up and took a sip. "Grudgingly I have to agree with you. Yes, let's do it. Did they give some dates they'd like to go? I'll have to get someone to cover for me at the sheriff's department, and you'll have to check with Roxie to see if she can manage Kelly's Koffee Shop during your absence for a few days."

Kelly swirled the coffee around in her "Boss Babe" mug, a gift from Roxie. "In her email Julia said that the crush, whatever that is, was recently finished, and that she'd like to go next week. Do you think that's too soon?"

"No, I think I can arrange something. And you?" he asked.

"Roxie mentioned the other day she'd seen a couch she'd like to buy, but she didn't feel she could justify the expense right now. This would probably help her, so I think it will work. I'll email Julia back and tell her we're 90% sure we can make it, but she better bring plenty of photographs, because Grandpa wants to see his girls." She grinned at Mike knowing what a sucker he was for his granddaughters.

"You've got that right." Mike squeezed Kelly's arm and stood up from the table, picking up his cell phone. "I'll make a couple of calls, and I should know whether or not it's a go in just a few minutes."

"I'll do the same before I email her and then we can give her a thumbs up or a thumbs down." She heard Mike talking on his phone in the hallway, while she placed a call to Roxie.

A few minutes later Mike walked back into the kitchen with a smile on his face after he'd called the sheriff's department. "I made it happen," he said. "I guess being the sheriff of Beaver County, Oregon, has its advantages when the sheriff wants a little time off to be with his wife. And you? How did it go?" he asked.

"Yes. Roxie's thrilled to have the chance to pick up some extra money. I'll email Julia right now and tell her it's a go."

"Great," Mike said, looking around. "While you're doing that, I'll start dinner. What did you have planned for tonight?"

"I wanted to make that recipe that's on the counter." Kelly motioned towards the open book on the recipe stand. "It's a Mexican salad with chicken. If it's any good, I thought I might be able to serve it at Kelly's. Go ahead and start. I'll be back in a few minutes."

She walked down the hall followed by their three dogs, Rebel, a large fawn boxer, Lady, a yellow Labrador retriever, and the newest addition to the Reynolds family, Skyy, a German shepherd who was almost out of puppyhood.

"Kelly, when you email Julia, tell her we'll fly into Sacramento, rent a car, and meet them in Sonoma," Mike called after her. "Also ask her where we should stay. I know it's kind of a sheriff thing, but I don't like to be dependent on someone else driving. Okay with you?"

Kelly smiled to herself. She was expecting it. "Sure," she said, "if it makes you happy, I'm all for it."

Julia must have been waiting for Kelly's answer because she responded to Kelly's email within minutes. Between them they worked out the arrangements for the following week. Kelly walked back into the kitchen after she finished with the last email. This time she was unaccompanied, as the dogs had left her as soon as they heard Mike opening kitchen cabinets and drawers, since they were always on the lookout for a treat or a dropped scrap of food.

"That pink apron suits you, Mike," she grinned. "It's all arranged.

We're meeting them next Monday at a bed and breakfast Julia's heard good things about. She'd already inquired as to availability and they have rooms available for both couples for three nights. Julia says the inn is about a block and a half from the Sonoma city square where there are lots of good restaurants."

Mike flipped the chicken in the skillet. "That sounds good, but I have to tell you that this is new territory for me. I've been to Napa and driven past the road that goes west to Sonoma, but I've never been there. How do we go about the wine tastings? Is Julia going to arrange for that?"

Kelly stepped beside her husband and inspected the chicken he was cooking. "Looks good. Yes, she said she would. She's called the Moretti Winery to see if we could have a private tour. From what Julia said, they only give private tours and unlike most other wineries, this one doesn't have a tasting room open to the public." Kelly started to chop the salad vegetables and munched on a piece of tomato before continuing.

"She'd tentatively made a reservation for the four of us for a private tour next Monday afternoon. I guess Julia had quite a conversation with the tour guide and they hit it off because both of them have passed some type of fancy schmancy wine test."

Kelly transferred the chopped tomatoes into the salad bowl. "Anyway, we're going to meet Julia and Brad at the bed and breakfast in the early afternoon and catch up. Julia said she checked and they have cars for hire in Sonoma, so she wants us to use one of them when we go wine tasting, which I think is smart. I'm not a big fan of going to a wine tasting and then getting in a car and driving, and knowing how you feel about drinking and driving, I didn't even bother to ask you. Whatever it costs, it's worth it."

"Couldn't agree more. Actually, the chicken is almost done. Why don't you set the table, and I can finish the salad? It's probably too late tonight, but tomorrow would you call the kennel and make a reservation for the dogs?" Mike turned down the heat on the chicken while Kelly pulled out silverware from a drawer.

MURDERED BY WINE

"I will," she said, as she moved across the room to the table. "But if you remember, Doc and Liz said they'd love to watch the dogs the next time we went out of town. They've got Lucky and Max, their new bulldog, and all five of the dogs have been together before. They have that big back yard that's fenced. Let's take them up on their offer. I think our dogs would love it."

"Fine with me, but that's a lot of dogs to take care of." Mike transferred the chicken to a large shallow bowl, while the dogs hovered around his feet in case anything might come their way.

"True, but after all Doc has been through these last few years, I think he's loving his new domesticated lifestyle, and what speaks more to a domesticated life than taking care of five dogs?"

"Not much. By the way, Kelly, I think you've got a hit on your hands with this salad. Let me get some iced tea and crackers to go with it, and I think we're good to go."

Mike plated the salads, served them, and then said, "Sit down and I'll make a toast to our new adventure." When they were both seated at the table, he lifted his glass, "To Sonoma and an enjoyable few days. We both can use the R and R, and I'm looking forward to it." They clicked their glasses and started to eat.

If murder makes for an enjoyable few days, then his toast was appropriate, but if not...

CHAPTER SIX

Shortly after noon on Monday of the following week, Mike drove north on Highway 12 towards Sonoma and a few minutes later he and Kelly saw the town square spread out before them. They'd done a little research and found out that the historic plaza had once been a Mexican military outpost, a frontier republic, a Spanish Mission village, and was now an historic landmark. On the far side of the square they saw the military outpost. The other three streets surrounding the square were packed with upscale restaurants, shops, wine bars, and everything else a desirable tourist destination would have. Conspicuous by their absence were any glitzy tee shirt shops or fast food chain restaurants.

In the newspaper Mike had read online, it was apparent that there was quite a battle taking place over whether the sleepy little town should remain as it is or open itself up to entrepreneurs who wanted to build large hotels and other businesses that catered to the tourist trade, particularly the people who came because of the area's renowned wine culture.

"Well, Kelly, what do you think?" Mike asked, slowing the car to a snail's pace.

"I think we've taken a step back in time. This is utterly charming, and who would think it would exist in the middle of a thriving wine industry that's becoming, from what Julia says, known throughout the world?"

"From that statement, I'm guessing that you're one of the people who would like to see it remain just like it is and not bow to the developers and others who want to see it become a much larger tourist attraction."

"I probably am." Kelly said as she gazed out the car window at the quaint scene that time appeared to have forgotten. "There's not much charm left in many of the areas that are destination tourist places. To see what could happen to Sonoma all you have to do is look at the neighboring Napa area which has bowed to commercial interests. That's just my opinion, and I'm sure it's a huge concern for the residents."

Mike peered through the windshield. "Would you double check me on where we're going? The instructions are in that file laying on the back seat. I think we go one block past the square and take a left. From what Julia wrote to us, the bed and breakfast should be located there."

A few minutes later Mike pulled into the driveway and followed the sign for Guest Parking. They both spent a moment looking at the large Queen Anne style home where they'd be staying for the next few days.

"Mike, it's beautiful and immaculate," Kelly said, as she admired the wooden building with its very distinctive style of architecture including a round tower at the top. "I love the large yard and all the flowers around the house and more hanging from baskets on the porch. It's utterly delightful. If our room is half as charming as what I'm seeing, I'm going to be very happy."

When they opened the front door, they were greeted by a young woman. "Welcome to the Sonoma Bed and Breakfast. My name is Brie. Since you have luggage, I'm assuming you'll be staying with us."

"Yes," Kelly said. "We have a reservation under the name of Reynolds."

The young woman checked her computer and said, "Here it is. I show Sheriff Mike and Kelly Reynolds. Is that right?"

"That's us. What do you need?"

"May I see a form of identification and the credit card you'll be using to pay for the room?"

"Certainly." A few moments later the young woman said, "You'll be staying in the Figueroa Room. Governor Figueroa was sent to Sonoma by the Mexican government in 1835 to protect the area from foreigners, particularly the Russians who were encroaching on the area north of San Francisco. Actually, it's my favorite room. Just go up the stairs, and it's the room at the end of the hall. I guess the reason I like it is because it's quite large. Most renovated Queen Anne homes have relatively small rooms."

"Thank you for your help," Kelly said, accepting the room key. "Our daughter and son-in-law will be here shortly. Would you let them know which room we're in?"

"Actually, your daughter called and requested that the Figueroa Room be reserved for you. She'd read about us on the Internet and found out it was our largest room. I remember talking to her, because I thought that was a very sweet thing for her to do."

"So do I," Kelly said. "I'm sure we'll enjoy it."

*****

"Mike, this is gorgeous." Kelly ran her hand across the polished wooden dresser. "Look, all the furniture appears to be period or very good reproductions."

"Have to say reproductions, sweetheart. Anytime you have a hole in the desk for a cell phone charger, I don't think it's authentic." Mike set the bags down and perched on the bed, bouncing up and down a few times to test it out.

"You're probably right, but those flowers in the yard are definitely real. This place is absolutely beautiful. And look, here's a bottle of wine and wine glasses. There's a note with it." She opened it and read, "To Mom and Dad. Looking forward to having a wonderful time with you. It's signed Julia and Brad. How sweet."

"I agree, and speaking of them, I think I just saw their car pull into the parking area," he said, walking across the room and looking out the window. "They'll probably be up here in a few minutes. Let's see if we can put a couple of things away, although it's definitely a plus that the room is large enough for a couple of chairs. We can all sit down for a few minutes. I wonder if they brought pictures of the girls."

"I think Julia knows how disappointed Grandpa would be if she didn't, so my bet is she did."

A few minutes later there was a knock on the door. "Julia, Brad, we've so been looking forward to this. Life in Calico Gold must agree with you, because you both look fantastic," Kelly said as she warmly embraced both of them. Mike walked over, kissed Julia, and shook hands with Brad.

"How are my girls?" Mike asked a few moments later. "I've been thinking about them a lot, and although I know this isn't the place for them, I miss them."

Julia exchanged a knowing smile with Kelly. "Tell you what, Mike, give us about twenty minutes or so to unpack and get organized, and I'll be back with a bunch of photos for you as well as some pictures they drew especially for you." She looked at her watch. "Our tour is set for 3:00 this afternoon, and I have a driver picking us up at 2:30. That gives us about an hour to catch up. Back in a few," Julia said as she and Brad walked out the door.

True to her word, twenty minutes later there was a knock on the door and Mike opened the door for them. Julia was holding a folder. "Okay Grandpa, sit down. Here's the latest from your little friends as well as some shots of the ranch, which I thought you'd like to see."

"Good grief, it never occurred to me that they'd be old enough to go into Brownies." Mike said as he began to leaf through the photos, handing them to Kelly after he'd seen them first. "Pretty soon they'll be off to college, and I will have missed it all."

Julia laughed. "Don't panic, Mike, I think we have a few years left before that happens. They're both very bright, but I don't think the colleges will be lining up in a year or two to give them an early admittance scholarship. Anyway, these are the photos of the girls. Also, here's one of Sam, the dog that was your aunt's," she said, pointing to it. "He's getting pretty old, so we got the girls a couple of puppies. Here's a picture of SamIAm and Samantha. They're border collies, and very good companions. True to their heritage, they herd the girls in the same fashion that they were bred to herd animals."

Mike looked over at Brad. "Speaking of animals, Brad, is John Wilson still renting part of the ranch as a pasture for his cattle?"

"Sure is, Mike, and we're still allowing him to get water from the stream that runs through the ranch. It works out well for both of us. We use the barn, a couple of acres of the land, and the greenhouse, and he's pretty much got the rest. Since it's our land, we can ride our horses wherever we want on it. And by the way, your granddaughters are getting to be quite the little horsewomen," Brad said as he puffed out his chest. "They've joined the local 4H club which has a branch that teaches horsemanship, and they've both won ribbons in a number of events they've entered. We're pretty proud of them."

Kelly's eyes shone with pride as she looked over at her daughter. "Sweetheart, you and Brad have to be the best parents in the world. And it's wonderful you were able to relocate and be the caretakers of the ranch Mike inherited when his Aunt Agnes was murdered. I think it's ever so much better than big city living," she said, giving her daughter a hug.

"Mom, the girls would agree ninety percent of the time, but right now the one thing they keep asking me with regularity is when we're going to take them to Disneyland. Quite frankly, it's never been number one on my list of things to do. I think they've heard too much from their friends and the media about it. Anyway, it will give them something to look forward to someday." Julia smiled and started putting the photos back in the folder.

"I think someday should come sooner rather than later," Mike said. "What do you say, Kelly? Why don't we take the girls to Southern California for a trip, and we'll go to Disneyland? We can rent a place on the beach, and they can play in the ocean as well."

Kelly looked at him open-mouthed. "Ummm, Mike, maybe we should discuss this later," she said in a low voice.

"Nope, I've made an executive decision." Mike slapped his hands on his knees. "If my granddaughters want to go to Disneyland, they're going to Disneyland, and you can tell them that, Julia. The only thing that needs to be decided is when."

"Well, so much for my input," Kelly said laughing. "Okay, I give. Disneyland here we come, at least here we come pretty soon."

Julia shared a smile with her husband before speaking, "Mike, Mom, I can't even begin to tell you how excited the girls are going to be when they hear about this. How about next summer? Doesn't make much sense to go to the beach and not be able to play in the water because of cool winter temperatures. How does that sound to both of you?"

"Sounds great," Mike said. "That will give us both plenty of time to get ready for it. As a matter of fact, I've never been to Disneyland, so this will be a first for me, too."

"Mom and I have," Julia said rolling her eyes, "but it was not one of my best memories. It was really hot when we went, and there were so many people. I remember trying to see everything that was going on at the Main Street Electric Parade, and I just got overwhelmed. I was glad when we got back to the hotel, but I was probably the only kid in the world who felt that way."

"Well, that works out perfectly, then," Mike said. "You have no desire to take them and I want to, so it's been decided. I think it's getting close to the time when the driver you hired is supposed to pick us up. We probably should go out in front, so we don't keep him waiting."

The four of them walked down the stairs and saw their hired car in the driveway waiting to take them to the Moretti Winery for the private tour Julia had arranged.

CHAPTER SEVEN

"Julia, this is a totally new experience for Mike and me," Kelly said as their hired car headed out of town towards the Moretti Winery. The roads were quiet as they sped past fields planted with row after row of grape vines for as far as they could see. "Are there some do's and don'ts we should be aware of?"

"From what I understand, this is a private tour, just the four of us. When I talked to the tour guide, she said she'd give us an overview, then take us out to the vineyard. She'll tell us some things about the grapes, etc., and then she said we would have a tour of the building where the wine is fermented, and we'd end up in their tasting room. She mentioned we'd be served a platter of appetizers with different kinds of cheese, nuts, and other things that would go well with the different wines we'll be tasting."

Kelly hesitated and then said, "Julia, would it embarrass you if I didn't drink much of the wines? Would that be considered a faux pas? I don't want to spoil the rest of my trip just because I have to do what's considered politically correct."

"Mom, if you'd ever been to a wine tasting, you'd know it's perfectly fine not to drink all of the wine that's poured for you," Julia assured her. "As a matter of fact, when you visit wine tasting rooms there's always a container to pour the wine you don't want into, and go on to the next one. They call it a "dump bucket" or "spit bucket" for a reason. I usually will just swirl a little around in my mouth and pour the rest of it out, however, given that this is a private tour it may be different. But no, don't feel that you have to drink all of it, and if one doesn't appeal to you, don't drink it."

"That makes me feel a lot better. Ever since I got your email I've been wondering how I could handle it."

"Looks like we're here," Brad said, pointing. "I see a sign for Moretti Winery over the gate up ahead." He turned to the driver and said, "We were told to just open the gate, and you could drop us off in the small parking lot next to the tasting room. The tour guide said it was the first building on the right. Thanks so much," Brad said as he counted out cash for the driver. "We'll see you back here at 5:15."

Julia opened the car door and said, "This is as beautiful as what we have in Calico Gold, although in a different way. Look at the acres of vineyards, really, about as far as the eye can see, and we couldn't have picked a more beautiful day."

The four of them walked across the parking lot and headed to the well-marked tasting room. On the walkway leading to the steps was a sign that said, "Welcome, Julia, Brad, Mike, and Kelly." When they got to the porch the door was opened by a very attractive middle-aged blond-haired woman wearing a white cowl-necked sweater, large gold hoop earrings, blue jeans and sandals. "Welcome to the Moretti Winery. My name is Josie Martin. Which one of you ladies is Julia?" she asked.

"That would be me. I'm the one you talked to. This is my husband, Brad, and my mother and father, Mike and Kelly Reynolds. As I told you on the phone, I teach classes on wine, so I am really excited to be here."

"Well, I'll do my best to make your time here worthwhile. Please, come in." They followed her into a large hallway with comfortable chairs. Off to one side was a room which looked like it had been set up for a wine tasting. Offices and a restroom led off of the hallway. She indicated for them to take a seat and handed each of them a glass of chilled white wine.

"As I show you different bottles of wine today, you'll notice that each one has a distinctive label, and that's because there is a story that goes with each one. The owner's wife, *Signora* Moretti, grew up on the family estate in Tuscany. The main house was a replica of a 16th century castle. She says some of her favorite memories were hiding from her nanny and her governess in the castle. She tells wonderful stories of the places she could get into that they couldn't. That's the reason for the staircase and the door under it depicted on the label of this bottle of wine. You'll notice that the label bears the name in quotes, '*Scala*' which means staircase in Italian.

"What you're drinking is a lovely smooth wine that's perfect for drinking before dinner or served with a fish entrée. It's also one of my favorites for having a glass of wine in the afternoon with friends. What do you think of it?" she asked.

"It's delicious," Julia said. "Is it readily available if I talk about it in my classes?"

"Julia, I apologize. When we spoke on the phone I told you I would give you some more advanced information on our wines, and I left the written materials I wanted to give you at my house. Is there any chance you could come back tomorrow and pick them up? I think you'll learn far more from that information than you will today. Given what you told me about the classes you've taken and the certificates you've earned, while the tour is always of interest, you'll probably be familiar with most of what I'll be telling you.

"But, in answer to your question, no, the Moretti wines are sold only during a tour, to members of the Moretti wine club, or at a few very high end restaurants here in Sonoma. We have a rather small vineyard, and our production is quite limited."

"Why is that?" Kelly asked. "I would think if the wines are popular the owners would want to produce as many bottles as possible."

"Generally that's true, Kelly, but this winery is a little different. Moretti is the name of the main vineyard located a few miles from here in Napa. It's quite large, and as a matter of fact, they buy grapes from smaller vineyards which don't have the capability to make their own wines. It's far more commercial than this winery. I'm sure you've seen Moretti wine in the local stores where you live. However, *Signor* Moretti wanted to experiment and see if he could produce award winning wines, and with this winery, he has."

"Josie, are you saying that all of the wines this winery produces are award-winning?" Mike asked with a raised eyebrow.

"Yes, that's exactly what I'm saying, but with a caveat. We only produce six different wines here. That allows for absolute quality control both in the vineyard and during the winemaking process. Come, it's time we go out to the vineyard, and I'll show you. Please, help yourself to more wine if you'd like to take a glass with you. After all, you paid for the tour," she said laughing.

For the next half-hour, Josie showed them the various different grape vines in the vineyard. She explained how the grapevines had originally been grafted, that the grafting process was ongoing, and that the grapes had all recently been handpicked by seasonal workers hired by Juan, the vineyard manager. She went on to explain that the picked grapes had been put through a sorting machine, destemmed and crushed, and the juice was then pumped into huge metal vats where the fermentation process takes place. Once the fermentation process was finished and the grape juice had been converted to wine, it was transferred to barrels for aging.

"I've heard that very few wineries handpick their grapes, because it's so labor intensive. Is that true?" Julia asked.

"Yes. Compared to a machine that goes down each row and grabs the clusters, handpicking is a very old method of selecting grapes. You'll notice that there are still some grapes on the vines. Those are the berries that the picker felt were not quite ready, so in addition to being labor intensive, Juan only hires pickers who know which grapes are ready to harvest and which ones aren't. The pickers will come back in another week or two and pick the remaining grapes. Our workers are paid well which is probably another reason why the Moretti wines from this winery are not cheap nor easily bought. Now it's time for me to take you to the vat barn and show you the room where the magic takes place. Please follow me."

CHAPTER EIGHT

They walked across the small parking lot to the building where Josie said the magic took place. Kelly noticed several homes beyond the building and curiously asked, "Josie, I see several homes spread out over there. Who lives in those?"

"We are very fortunate here at the Moretti Winery. *Signor* Moretti wanted to hire the best people he could for his boutique winery and as an inducement, he offered to let them live rent free in a house located here on the premises. I live in the one on the right, Jim Barstow, the manager of all that takes place here, lives in the center one, and the far one to the left is the home of Angela and Matteo Lucci. Angela is the winemaker for the winery, and I would have to say, probably the best winemaker in the valley. She and her husband worked for the Moretti family at their vineyards in Tuscany, Italy."

"Wow, I didn't know that the staff at wineries had perks like that," Brad said.

"Mostly, they don't," Josie replied. "As a matter of fact, I believe this is the only winery in Napa or Sonoma where it's done. And the homes are not small. I have three bedrooms, so when my son and daughter come to visit, there's still plenty of room for them. *Signor* Moretti felt that when the staff is being fairly compensated, they will do a better job, and I think he's right."

The doors on the large building were slightly ajar and Josie motioned for them to join her as she stepped into the building. They walked into an expansive room, which was dominated by six large twenty-foot-tall stainless-steel vats and beyond the vats hundreds of wooden barrels were stacked in rows, one on top of the other, four high.

"This is where everything takes place. We call this building the vat barn. The vats are filled with raw grape juice which is allowed to ferment and turn into wine. Then it's transferred to barrels when Angela decides it's time. You'll notice several kinds of wooden barrels. Each type of oak barrel imparts a different character to the wine. Angela also decides which barrels she wants to use and what percentage of the different kinds of the grape juice should be blended into each vat to create the desired type of wine. It's a very exacting process and obviously, she's very good at what she does.

"A sample of wine is taken each morning and sent to a laboratory in Sonoma for analysis. Additionally, Angela takes a tiny taste from the vats each evening. Once the wine is transferred to the barrels, it won't be disturbed until it comes time to bottle it."

"How does someone take a tiny taste from something as large as that vat?" Mike asked.

"Very carefully. You can see that the vats are covered by a fitted metal lid at the top. There is a latch which can be released to allow the lid to open. Angela dips a tiny wooden cup attached to a long metal handle into the vat to get the sample. The wine in the vat gives off a huge amount of carbon dioxide as it ferments, and it can be lethal if someone places their face over the open lid for too long of a time. Every year there are stories of people falling into wine vats and dying after they have accidentally inhaled an overdose of carbon dioxide."

"It's probably inappropriate to say what a way to go," Brad said laughing.

"Probably so," Josie answered. "You'd never think something like that could happen to people who are knowledgeable about wine, but several years ago a Spanish woman who was a wine specialist was taking a sample from one of the fermentation tanks where she worked, and she fell into it and died. What was even more tragic was that her uncle, who was the owner of the vineyard, was the one who discovered her." She shook her body in mock horror. "Just the thought of it is enough to keep me from ever taking a sip from one of the vats."

"Are the wines in these vats stirred?" Julia asked.

"Rarely. Angela prefers to let the lees, or the yeast deposit, sink to the bottom of the vats and remain there. She doesn't like that much yeast to be released into the wine itself." Josie looked at her watch and said, "I see we're running a little late and it's time for our wine tasting. Please, follow me up the stairs to the wine tasting room."

The four of them, along with Josie, walked into a bright and airy room with large windows looking out at the beautiful Moretti vineyard. An aged rectangular dark wooden table had been set for four people. In front of each person were five wine glasses, each filled with a different wine. Small individual platters containing different kinds of cheese, fruits, and crackers were also placed invitingly before them. Between the wine glasses and the platter was a printed legend describing each wine and which cheese, fruit and cracker best complemented it. A glass of chilled water was located to the right of the wine glasses.

"These are the premier wines from the Moretti Winery," Josie explained, as they settled themselves at the table. "I'll be telling you a little about each of them, and please feel free to ask me questions. I urge you to taste not only the wine but also the suggested foods that best accompany them, and please, don't pass up the chocolate which is paired with the last wine. It's specially made for our winery with a little of the wine that accompanies it actually being one of the ingredients in it."

For the next hour, they listened intently as Josie told them about the wines. They tested, tasted, and tried the various wines and accompaniments. True to her word, Kelly only had one small sip of each of the different kinds of wine, but managed to eat everything on her platter. The cheeses had her mouth watering for more.

"Josie, I have a question, but it's not wine related. Where do these wonderful cheeses come from? Really, they're the best I've ever had."

"Thank you, Kelly. We get our cheese from two local artisanal cheese makers. I'll be happy to give you their names and how to contact them. Actually, when Julia comes by tomorrow to pick up the wine information I have for her, I'll put that information with hers. There's a wonderful shop on the square in Sonoma where you can buy these cheeses, but I'm told you can also order them online."

"Thank you so much. I own a coffee shop in Oregon, and I would love to have a cheese platter on the menu, although I have a feeling it wouldn't be very cost effective."

"I don't know. Maybe you can get it wholesale. I don't order what's served here, so maybe Jim buys it wholesale. The one thing I can tell you is that the chocolates are not available to the public. They're made exclusively for our winery. Aren't they wonderful?"

Nodding heads affirmed they were all in agreement. "I don't want to rush you, but we've gone over our two-hour allotted time limit, and I saw a car pull into the parking lot which I imagine is for you," Josie said as she glanced outside. "If you do wish to buy a bottle of wine or join our wine club, please let me know, and I can process your request. Thank you so much for spending time here at the Moretti Winery, and Julia, I'll see you tomorrow."

CHAPTER NINE

"Well, Mom, Mike, what did you think of the Moretti Winery?" Julia asked as they rode back to town. She was holding on her lap the two bottles of wine she'd bought, which had been safely packed in a signature wine bag with the initials, M and W, intertwined in the form of grape vines.

"I thought it was fascinating. I found out more in the two hours we were with Josie than I've known about wine in my entire life. I guess I'm a real lightweight, because there was no way I could drink all the glasses of wine we were given at the tasting. One sip of each was enough for me. Thanks for arranging it, sweetheart," Kelly said, settling back into the soft leather seat of the car they'd hired.

Julia smiled, clearly pleased with Kelly's response. "I guess I'm the designated tour guide for our trip, because I made reservations for Brad and Mike to play golf at the Sonoma Golf Club tomorrow morning. I have a friend who has an in there, and I was able to get you two on the course as guests of a member. It's quite famous and in the past, has hosted the PGA Champions Tour. You have an 8:00 a.m. tee time.

"Mom, I thought we could have a leisurely breakfast, then head back to the Moretti Winery, so I can pick up the information Josie has for me. After that we can do some shopping. From what I researched on the Internet, it looks like there are some great shops on the square, and Mom, I even located a cooking specialty store for you."

Mike scratched his head, and with a sideways look at Brad said, "I rarely play golf, so if you don't want me to embarrass you, I'd understand. You can play by yourself, and I'll accompany Kelly and Julia."

"Sorry, Mike, you're not getting off that easy," Brad said in an easygoing tone of voice. "I checked after Julia made the reservation, and they have clubs for rent. From what the man at the pro shop said, there's rarely anybody on the course that early on a weekday, so we should have it to ourselves. I don't play that much myself, so no one will be around to make fun of us duffers."

Kelly elbowed Mike. "Mike, you should definitely do that. You rarely have a free day, and I think it would be good for you. Plus, we couldn't ask for more beautiful weather. Enjoy, and I really would like to spend a little time with our daughter," Kelly said as she smiled at Julia.

"Okay, if you promise I won't ruin your time on the course, I'd enjoy it. Julia, thanks for making the reservation. This comes as a complete surprise."

"I figured there was no way Mom could do wine tasting every day, so this seemed like a good idea. Golf for you two and retail therapy for us. Now, about tonight." Julia looked around the car, and three expectant pairs of eyes stared back at her. "I made reservations at an Italian restaurant which is supposed to be fabulous, and it's only half a block off the square in our direction. We can walk to it. Let's go back to the bed and breakfast, relax, and meet up for our 7:30 reservation about 7:15 in the parlor room by the front door. Sound okay?"

"Sounds great, and I might even indulge in a nap," Mike said grinning. "The combination of wine and cheese made me sleepy, and the bed is nice and soft. I'll have just enough time for a quick snooze. If I'm expected not to make a fool of myself in the morning on the golf course, I might as well get as much rest as I can."

*****

Promptly at 7:15, they set off for Angelo's Restaurant, touted as one of the best Italian restaurants in the Sonoma area. A few minutes later the four of them were seated in the secluded patio area. The evening was cool, and outdoor heaters warmed the air. They were surrounded by lush plants and flowers that defied the season, their fragrance intermingling with strains of violin music and twinkling lights to create an intimate ambiance.

"I don't know if I've ever been in a restaurant with such a romantic feeling," Kelly said. "Julia, if the food is half as good as the atmosphere, I'll be happy."

Mike cleared his throat. "Kelly, if there's one thing I like to hear you say it's that something is putting you in a romantic mood. Please, hold the thought."

"Mike, you're incorrigible, but I will hold the thought just for you," she said as she smiled at him with an encouraging look of promise in her eyes.

Brad shuffled his menu while Julia piped up, "Hey you two lovebirds, we're the somewhat newlyweds around here and just think, we have two more days to explore this area. I love it here. Thanks again for joining Brad and me." She dipped a piece of freshly baked bread in a dish of olive oil and balsamic vinegar. She swallowed and closed her eyes. "Good grief, Mom, you have to try this. It's fabulous, and it's something you could serve at Kelly's."

Kelly tore off a small piece of bread from the warm loaf, dipped it and said, "I agree. It's wonderful, and a new bakery has just come in town. I'll bet I could get them to deliver a couple of loaves a day and see how it goes."

"If you want my opinion, Kelly, and I'm sure you do," Mike said, "I think you better up your order to several loaves. This is fabulous.

Be my bet that everyone who tries it will want it the next time they come in. You could even have Roxie bring it out at lunch right after she gives your customers their menus." He reached for a second piece.

"I think it's unanimous, Mom, this would be delicious at the coffee shop. So, what's everyone having for dinner? I'll start, because I read the menu before I came. The chicken breast stuffed with mushrooms, cheese, and herbs is definitely calling to me."

"Pappardelle with prosciutto in a cream sauce sounds delicious," Kelly said as she reached for her purse.

"Kelly, please don't make a scene in the restaurant by taking a photo of the dish with your cell phone. Just enjoy the experience for once. There's nothing wrong with leaving your work at home," Mike said sternly.

"All right, if you insist, although I wasn't thinking of making it for the coffee shop, I was thinking of making it for us."

"Well, in that case, I suppose one or two photos would be okay," Mike said sheepishly. "Just try and keep it very low key."

"Mike, in case you haven't noticed," Julia said, "everyone takes pictures of their food nowadays, and then they put it on Instagram or Pinterest. It's kind of the 'in' thing to do. Believe me, Mom won't stand out at all."

"It's called food porn," Brad informed Mike, who looked perplexed.

"Hmmm, I see. I suppose you're right, Julia. Call it an age thing," Mike said with a grunt. "So as far as dinner goes, I've decided on the sea bass." He snapped his menu shut. "I love it, and you don't see it all that often on the menu."

"Risotto for me," Brad said. "It's pretty time consuming to make and something we never have at home." He turned to Julia, "And I'm not suggesting that you stop taking care of the girls, the ranch, the wine classes, and everything else you do, just to spend an hour standing over the stove stirring something for me," he said grinning.

They were all talking about how wonderful the dinner had been when the waiter approached their table carrying a tray of desserts. "I'm sorry, but you must have the wrong table. We were so full we decided not to order any dessert," Kelly said.

"The chef is testing out a new dessert tonight, and all of the diners are getting a chance to try it. It's complementary, but he would like to know what you think of it," he said as he placed a small cup that looked like it was made of chocolate with a liquid inside in front of each of them. "It's a chocolate cup with a little sparkling wine it. He thinks it would make a nice accompaniment to the tiramisu, which is pretty much our signature dessert here. First you drink the sparkling wine in the cup, and when it's all gone, you cut up the chocolate cup and eat it. Enjoy!"

The four of them began eating with ill-disguised gusto. "The things we have to do to help the chef," Mike muttered, but devouring his chocolate cup in just a couple of bites.

A few minutes later the waiter returned to their table and said, "Well, how was your chocolate experience?"

"It was absolutely one of the best things I've ever had, and how clever of him," Kelly said. "I've never seen that done anywhere, and I'm a big fan of the cooking shows on television as well as an avid reader of food magazines. Please, tell the chef that these are definitely worth serving. People will probably start ordering dessert before their main entrees when the word gets out."

"That I doubt, but I will definitely tell the chef that you approve," he nodded. "Here's your bill, and thank you for coming to Angelo's. We hope you'll return soon.

When the bill had been settled, they decided a walk back to the bed and breakfast. A short walk and a good night's sleep would finish off the day perfectly, and so it did. Little did they know it was the calm before the storm.

CHAPTER TEN

At 6:00 the next morning, the phone in Mike and Kelly's room rang. It was on Kelly's side of the bed, and she groggily reached for it. "Hello," she said, wondering who could possibly be calling at that hour. The only people she'd given the bed and breakfast number to had been Doc and Liz, who were taking care of their dogs and Roxie, who was managing Kelly's Koffee Shop in her absence. A call from either of them was not a good thing at this hour of the morning.

"Mom, it's me," Julia said. "I'm sorry to call so early, but we have a bit of an emergency, and we're leaving for home in a few minutes."

"What's wrong?" Kelly asked, sitting up in bed, wide awake, every motherly nerve of hers on high alert. "Is something wrong with you or Brad?"

"No. I didn't want to worry you yesterday, but Ella had a bit of a fever when we left home. She tends to run them occasionally, so I wasn't too concerned. But we got a call from the woman who's staying with them, and now we're both concerned. She's running a temperature of 103 degrees. I told Nancy, the woman who's staying with them, that we'd be home shortly. It's early enough if we leave now we can beat the rush hour traffic, so we should be home in a little over two hours. Depending on how she's doing, we'll either take her into emergency, or I'll get her in to see her pediatrician as soon as possible."

Mike rolled over as Kelly whispered her reply. "Oh, honey, I'm so sorry. Can we do anything to help?"

"I wish you could, but she needs her mommy and daddy. It will probably be one of those times when we get home the temperature will be gone and she'll be fine, but we can't risk it. As a matter of fact, you could do me a favor. I told Josie I'd pick up the wine information she was gracious enough to put together for me, so if you could get it from her, that would be a big help."

"No problem. I'll send it to you. Give Ella a hug and a kiss from us. Actually, better do the same to Olivia. I don't want to be the cause of any sisterly jealousy."

"I will," Julia said laughing. "Wait a minute. Brad's saying something." It was quiet for a moment, then Julia said, "Brad says to tell Mike to go ahead and play golf. He'll probably have the course to himself, and it's supposed to be absolutely beautiful. He said please cancel his reservation. Mom, I really do have to go. Love you, and I'll call you when I know more." The phone went dead.

"I heard everything," Mike said, opening his eyes. "I hope Ella's going to be all right. That sounds like an awfully high fever. Do you think we should drive over there?"

"No. Kids can spike really high fevers, and then they'll go back to normal in a matter of hours, but Julia's right. You can't ignore it. It could be something a little more serious. Fortunately, they're not all that far from their home in the Sierra foothills. I'm thinking since we're already awake we can have breakfast, and then I'll take you to the golf course." Kelly looked at him as he made a face. "I'll wait an hour or so and then go out to the winery and pick up the information Josie said she'd have for us. You can call me when you're through playing golf. Since you're starting so early and probably playing by yourself, it shouldn't take all that long, and then we can have a late lunch and do whatever."

Mike stretched his arms and silently yawned. "Well, I just hope I don't have to play with anyone. I'm strictly a duffer, and it wouldn't have bothered me to play with Brad, but I think I'd be totally intimidated if I was playing with a couple of really good golfers."

"You can always say you don't feel good. Just make sure you get your own cart. That way you can head back to the clubhouse and call me. I can be there to pick you up in just a few minutes."

Mike squinted his eyes and said, "Yeah, having my own cart is kind of like having my own car when we go someplace, like here. The way it's turned out, it's a good thing I said we'd rent a car rather than have Brad and Julia pick us up at the airport."

"To change the subject, why don't you let me take my shower first?" Kelly said. "I take a lot longer getting dressed than you do."

"Darling, I'd never noticed. I see that someone put a newspaper under our door, so I'll read what's going on in the world while you make yourself beautiful."

"Spoken like a true diplomat," she said as she leaned over, kissed him, and then walked into the bathroom.

*****

Later when they pulled up in front of the traditionally styled clubhouse at the Sonoma Golf Club, Kelly said, "Mike, if the golf course is half as beautiful as the clubhouse, you're in for a treat, plus it has to be one of the most beautiful fall days I've ever seen."

She eyed the rolling terrain accented by massive oak tree and could see a lake off in the distance. The course overlooked the sweeping Mayacamas mountains and neighboring vineyards. If Kelly hadn't promised to pick up the papers for Julia, she might have been tempted to take up golf for herself for one day. "Forget about whatever you have going on back in Cedar Bay and just enjoy yourself. I'll wait for your call."

"You're sure you'll be okay driving out to the Moretti Winery?"

"Yes, this car has a GPS, and I pretty much remember how we went yesterday. It's not all that far."

"Okay. Please tell Josie again how much we enjoyed the tour and how much we learned." He leaned over and kissed her as he opened the door. "Wish me luck. Not many things make me nervous at this stage of my life, but the prospect of playing golf with two scratch golfers might just do it."

"Love you and see you later," she said. She watched Mike saunter over to the pro shop as she waved and drove away.

CHAPTER ELEVEN

Carlos Romano was sitting in his office at the Romano Winery, talking to his winemaker, Matteo Lucci. He rubbed his unshaven chin. "Matteo, what can we do to make our wines better? I'm at the end of my rope. It's so frustrating to see the Moretti Winery get all the top awards every year, and we come in second. Since the crush is over and we have a little time before we bottle the wine, do you have any ideas?"

"Carlos, I wish I did." Matteo said as he studied Carlos' lined and weathered face. Carlos had always been patient, waiting for Matteo to produce an award-winning wine, and Matteo sensed he was getting tired of Matteo failing to produce the results he wanted. "Believe me, there is nothing I want more than to be known as the winemaker of the top wines produced in the valley. The vines here are good, and we don't have a problem with disease or contaminates. Quite frankly, I just don't know why we are not able to capture the top awards."

Carlos continued to press the point. "Don't you and your wife ever discuss it? I mean, she's the winemaker for the winery that gets the top awards, and you're her husband. Doesn't she ever share with you what she does? How different can it be from what we do?" He raked a hand through his gray shoulder length hair in frustration.

"No, we don't discuss it. It infuriates me Angela makes better wine than I do. Trust me, I really want to be the best winemaker in the valley, but as long as she's around, I don't know how that's going to happen." Matteo's posture was hunched, sharing Carlos' frustration. "And I have no idea what she does that makes her wines just that much better. It was causing so much friction between us, she finally told me she would never again discuss the subject with me."

Carlos eyed him with concern. "I can understand that. I'm sure it would be the cause of some marital tension. Is there anything you can think of that she does differently from us?"

Matteo was quiet for several moments, his chin resting in his hand, then he spoke. "The only thing I know of that she does differently than we do is that every day she takes a sip of each of the wines that are fermenting in the vats after the crush. She does it every night promptly at 7:00 p.m. I know the exact time because we have dinner after that, but I don't see what that has to do with producing good wine."

Carlos frowned. "I don't either, but it must have something to do with it." Just then there was a knock on the door. "Come in," Carlos said, pausing to see who was entering. "Aah, Alessandra, what can I do for you?" Carlos didn't miss the lingering glance Matteo gave her and couldn't blame him. If she wasn't his niece, he'd probably do the same. Nor did he miss the flirtatious look she gave Matteo.

It was hard not to feel carnal longings for the sultry looking twenty-seven-year-old dark-haired Italian beauty with pouty lips and a body even movie stars would envy. She was dressed in a low-necked fitted red sweater that showed off her ample cleavage. Tight jeans and a wide tightly clenched belt highlighted her small waist and long legs. She wore a pair of rubber-soled sandals with dark blue socks, which seemed out of place with the rest of her outfit.

She was spending a year with Carlos, learning the ways of American wine-making, so she could take what she learned back to her family in Tuscany. It was obvious from the way Matteo was looking at her with undisguised lust that whatever Alessandra was feeling, Matteo was feeling the same way. An idea began to form in Carlos' mind.

"Please join us, Alessandra. We were just talking about what Matteo could do to become the number one winemaker in the valley, but I am curious why you are wearing sandals now that summer is over."

"I like to wear them when I'm out in the vineyard. It's not that cold and it's so easy to wash the dirt off, as well as the mud, if we've had some rain. From what I've seen, most of the winemakers wear them. See, Matteo has them on. I think you're about the only one who doesn't wear them.

"Anyway, Uncle Carlos, I came to talk to you about Angela as well," she said as she looked over at Matteo behind eyelashes as thick as a camel's. "I have spent time with many of the wine people here in the valley since I came to live with you, and almost all of them wonder how Angela continues to turn out the best award-winning wines, considering the small size of the Moretti Winery. Some say she's a witch and casts a magic spell over the vines."

Carlos turned and looked at Matteo. "Maybe that's the secret we've been looking for, Matteo. Who knows? It could be that you're married to a witch." He laughed. "Many years ago in Italy, if someone was thought to be or accused of being a witch, they were killed. And just think, what if Angela had an accident, and I mean a really bad accident? Certainly, accidents have been known to happen to witches. What if she fell in one of the vats while she was doing her nightly tasting? It would be a tragedy, of course."

He created a steeple with the fingers of his hands and continued, "But then again, if there were to be an accident of that nature, you would become, by default, the number one winemaker in the valley."

Matteo looked at him in disbelief. "Carlos, that is crazy talk, and I don't want to hear any more of it."

Carlos looked at him with an innocent expression on his face and said, "Matteo, I'm not suggesting anything. I was only saying what a tragedy it would be if something happened to Angela, but then again, as a consequence, you would be the number one winemaker in the valley."

Matteo was quiet for a long time, and then he began to speak. "My grandmother believed in witches and Satan. She was always telling us that she was glad that we three boys were right-handed because left-handed people made the sign of the cross with that hand, and everyone knew that Satan used his left hand to baptize witches. She said that anyone who was left-handed was a witch, and she said they should all be killed." He took a deep breath and said, "Angela is left-handed."

Following that remark, the silence in the room was deafening. They looked at one another, but none of them wanted to break the silence. Finally, Matteo stood up and said, "I must go. It is late. I want to forget this conversation ever happened, but I probably won't be able to." He closed the door behind him as he walked out of the room.

When he was gone, Carlos turned towards Alessandra and said, "It is obvious you have feelings for Matteo. Would I be right?"

Alessandra's face lit up as she spoke. "Yes, Uncle Carlos, from the moment I met him, I felt something here." She raised a hand to her chest and continued to speak. "But he is married. It is stupid of me, I know, but I often make up excuses to go to his office, or out in the vineyards if he is there, or visit the tasting room in the hope that he will be there. It is hopeless. I have never had a problem getting a man to fall in love with me, but Matteo is different."

Carlos pondered what she had just said. "Maybe not so much. It seems to me the problem is his wife. If she were no longer around, you would not have a problem getting Matteo to be yours. If she were to have an accident when she was having her evening sip of wine from the vats…" His voice drifted off as he locked eyes with his beautiful niece, who was lost in thoughts of her own.

CHAPTER TWELVE

"Nadia, come join me, and we can sit on the veranda. It's a beautiful evening, and I want to share a bottle of our best wine with you. After all we, deserve it," Giovanni Moretti said to his wife of twenty-five years.

The last rays of the sun bathed the nearby hills in a soft glow as the vineyards of the Moretti wine holdings stretched out as far as the eye could see. Giovanni's family had been important members of the wine industry in Italy for over a century and after many family discussions, it was decided that it was time for the Moretti family to expand their winemaking business in the Napa-Sonoma region of California. The family had purchased sixty acres, and Giovanni had come to California and planted the grape vines that had done so well in Tuscany.

Within a few years, the Moretti label became one of the best known in the young California wine industry, and the name was one to be trusted for quality and excellence. In addition to the vines he had brought with him from Italy, he added to the family of Moretti wines by buying grapes from many nearby smaller vineyards and used them to create blends that were less expensive, but well received by the thirsty public.

After several years, he felt it was time to marry, and his family was insistent that he wed a woman named Nadia who was the daughter of the owner of a neighboring vineyard in Tuscany. When his family mentioned her name, he remembered how beautiful she was. One year he returned to Italy for the Christmas holidays and two months later returned with Nadia as his bride It was a decision he never regretted, although after a meaningless affair he'd had early in their marriage, she made it very clear to him, family and religion notwithstanding, that if it ever happened again, she would leave him. She even hinted that might be the least of his problems with his death being another option.

Many times over the years, her fear of him having another affair had led to fiery arguments, but true to his word, he had never strayed from his marriage after that one time. Even so, he knew it was never far from her mind. It was like the elephant in the room that no one wanted to acknowledge, something that was always in the back of the temperamental Nadia's mind.

"This is excellent, Gio. I assume it's from our winery in Sonoma. I think you made a very good decision when you decided to purchase the Sonoma vineyard and plant it with the best grapes money could buy. The wine that is made there is excellent. No wonder we win awards for it every year."

"That's true, *caro mio*, but I wonder how successful we would be without Angela. She really is the best winemaker in the valley. We are so fortunate to have her. When my parents suggested we hire her for our new undertaking, the Moretti Winery, it was a very good decision. I'm certainly glad they urged me to do so."

After several moments, Gio became aware that Nadia had not spoken, and there was a scowl on her face. "*Caro mio*, what is it? Is something wrong? Is it something I've said or done?" he asked as he gently swirled the wine in his glass to release the bouquet.

"Gio, you don't need to say or do anything. It's rather obvious that the fact that Angela is responsible for the excellent wine we produce is a plus, but the real reason you keep her is that you can't take your eyes off of her whenever you're around her, and it has nothing to do with the wine." Nadia sighed, setting her wine glass down on the marble tabletop. "This has lost its appeal for me."

"Nadia, that's not fair. I have never given you one reason to think anything like that. We put that subject to rest years ago, and I thought we'd agreed to never discuss it again."

Nadia sighed again, a sad smile crossing her face, but her eyes betrayed the smile with their anger. "You agreed never to discuss it again. How stupid do you think I am?" She hissed at him. "I know it's just a matter of time until you and Angela have an affair. You think I don't know she'd much rather be the wife of the owner of the prestigious Moretti Winery rather than married to her husband, a second-rate winemaker.

"All the men talk about how beautiful she is, and I'm sure that her beauty, along with her winemaking excellence, will prove irresistible to you. It's just a matter of when." Nadia leaned across the table waving her hand at Giovanni, who shrunk back. "Maybe it's time for me to handle the situation. You never were a man who could resist a temptation, and if the temptation was no longer around..." She jutted her chin out, her mouth set firmly in a straight line.

"Nadia, quit talking like a crazy woman. The only relationship I have with Angela is one of business, nothing more."

"Really?" Nadia's brow creased. "I seem to remember you saying those very same words many years ago. It looks like history is going to repeat itself in the form of Angela Lucci. Well, not if I have anything to say about it. Everyone knows that after the crush she has a little sip from the vats at 7:00 p.m. every night. It would truly be a shame if she fell into one of the vats when she was tasting the wine. I'm going to bed. I have a headache. Good night, Gio," she said as she strode off the veranda and slammed the door shut behind her.

CHAPTER THIRTEEN

Kelly returned to the bed and breakfast after she'd taken Mike to the Sonoma Golf Club and spent an hour reading a book she'd had on her Kindle for months. She could easily have spent another hour or so in the comfortable guest lounge that housed an assortment of comfortable mismatched armchairs and walls of books and art pieces, but she promised herself she would return later with Mike. Josie had told them the previous afternoon that she was always in her office by 9:30, so Kelly was sure she'd be there by now.

Between the GPS and her memory, she had no problem driving to the Moretti Winery, but when she got there she was surprised to see a number of vehicles, including sheriffs' cars. The gates to the vineyard were wide open, and she was easily able to park her car in the parking lot. She opened her car door and glanced over at the barn where the wine vats were located. She gasped involuntarily when she saw the yellow tape surrounding it, indicating it was the scene of a crime. She hurried up the steps leading to the tasting room and office area, while a number of law enforcement personnel milled around the area.

Kelly walked down the hall to Josie's office and knocked on the door. "Come in," a tearful voice said as a dog barked on the other side of the door. "Don't worry, the dog won't hurt you."

A worried Kelly opened the door and saw Josie cuddling an adorable little dog who was madly licking her face. It was easy to see the dog was trying to lick away her tears.

"Josie, I'm sorry. I had no idea there has been some sort of a problem here at the winery. If this isn't a convenient time, I can come back later," Kelly said as she turned back towards the open door.

"No, it's fine, Kelly," Josie said as she waved her in. "As a matter of fact, I could do with the company right now. Please come in. You'll hear about it soon enough on the television news or read about it in the paper, so I might as well be the one to tell you."

"Tell me what? Hear about what?" Kelly sat down opposite Josie, who continued to cuddle the dog.

"Remember the winemaker who came into the tasting room yesterday? Her name was Angela Lucci. I introduced her, and she talked to your group for a moment or so."

Kelly nodded.

"I heard a lot of barking yesterday evening," Josie sniffed. "I recognized it as Angela's dog, this little girl, Foxie, is her name." She stroked Foxie's head while she laid very still on her lap. "She's such a lovable little fox terrier, and Angela had told me that although the breed was known for barking, she'd trained her not to, but when I heard her it was almost as if she was frantic. I was in my house, and the barking went on and on. Finally, I decided something might be wrong, so I went in the direction of the sound of her barking."

Josie's lip quivered and her shoulders shook. "It was coming from the vat barn. The doors were slightly ajar and Foxie was on a leash tied to a nearby post and looking in, all the time trying to shake her leash off.

"I calmed her down, and then I went into the barn. I didn't see anything, but I noticed that the lid on the first fermentation vat was open. Angela was very firm that the lids should be secured at all times, because she didn't want contaminants of any type to get into the vats."

"What happened?" Kelly asked.

"I walked up the steps of the vat where the lid was open, looked down into the vat, and saw Angela's body floating in the wine. She was dead." Josie began to sob uncontrollably, covering her face with her hands while Foxie made whimpering sounds.

It took Kelly a moment to digest what Josie had just told her. From what she had seen of Angela the previous afternoon, the woman had seemed pleasant, and nothing about her had struck Kelly as out of the ordinary. "Oh, Josie, what a tragedy. What do you think happened?"

"Well, as I said on the tour yesterday, every year we hear stories about someone who becomes overwhelmed by carbon dioxide fumes, falls in a wine vat, and dies. I think I even mentioned the case in Spain where the winery owner's niece fell in a vat and died, but Angela was the most careful person I've ever met. I just don't see that happening to her."

"What a horrible thing to discover. Did you call the sheriff or what?"

"Not right away. I went to Jim's home and told him what I'd discovered. He hurried down to the barn with Foxie and me. I'd taken Foxie with me when I left the barn, and Jim confirmed I was right, that Angela was dead. As the manager, it was his responsibility to call the sheriff, and he did. Within minutes, the place was swarming with the sheriff, his deputies, firemen, paramedics, all kinds of emergency response people, and later the coroner."

"Angela was married, wasn't she?"

"Yes, her husband is the winemaker at the Romano Winery."

"How did he take it?"

"Jim and I went to their home after the police had been called. We felt that we owed it to him to tell him before the police interviewed him."

"How did he do?"

"He wasn't home when we got there. In the meantime, the sheriff had arrived, and he was the one who told Matteo the said news. It was horrible. Matteo appeared to be devastated. I kept Foxie because she isn't Matteo's favorite, and he had enough on his mind without having to deal with a dog that had been devoted to his wife, who was now dead. Matteo and Foxie never really bonded. I'd like to think Matteo was devastated, but then again…" Josie looked off in the distance, as her voice trailed away.

"I'm sorry, I didn't hear you," Kelly said.

"It was nothing," Josie said.

She was quiet for several moments and then she said, "Angela was a friend of mine. Actually, she was my closest friend. We shared a love of wine and everything about it. She was a wonderful person, and I'm going to miss her so much." She started to cry again.

"You don't think she accidentally fell into the wine vat, do you?" Kelly asked. "Maybe she was distracted by something or slipped."

"No, I don't think she accidentally fell in," Josie said in a very firm voice. "As I said, Angela was extremely careful about everything having to do with wine. That's why Foxie was tied up. She wouldn't let her into the vat barn when she took her nightly sip, because she didn't want any dog hair to get in the wine. No, there is no way Angela just fell into the vat."

"Were there any signs of trauma on her body?"

"None," Josie said.

"Do you think foul play may have been involved in her death?"

Kelly asked, her eyes narrowing.

Josie spoke without hesitation. "I shouldn't say this, but I think someone wanted her dead. I think she was pushed into the vat."

"Good grief. What a horrible way to go. I'm sure there are some people who are anti-alcohol who would feel it was a fitting end for a winemaker, but that seems pretty extreme. If she was pushed into the wine vat, who do you think could have done it? Did she have any enemies?"

Josie stroked Foxie while she contemplated Kelly's question. The little dog began to yelp and struggled to break out of her grasp.

"I'm not in law enforcement, Josie, although as you may remember, my husband is," Kelly began to explain. "I've found myself involved in a number of murder investigations, and maybe I can be of help. My husband always says that nothing is too small to be overlooked. Actually, I'm kind of at loose ends for the next couple of days. Perhaps we could be of help if Angela's death was not an accident, as you seem to think."

Josie loosened her grip on Foxie, who wriggled away and onto the floor where she sniffed around Kelly's feet. "Table that for a minute," Josie said, standing up, and for the first time since Kelly had arrived, her face relaxed. "I need to use the restroom. I'll be right back."

CHAPTER FOURTEEN

A few moments later Josie returned from the restroom. Her face still had several drops of water on it, and she'd applied some lipstick, evidence that she'd tried to wash her face and achieve some semblance of control.

"Somehow washing my face with cold water always makes me feel better," Josie said.

Kelly noted she appeared more composed, although there was still an air of sadness around her. "Yes, I've always said that once I have my morning shower, I can take on about anything. Anyway, before you left, I asked you if Angela had any enemies."

"I wouldn't say she had any commonly known enemies, but Angela was well known in the valley for her winemaking abilities. You can't be the brains behind the best wine in the valley and not make some enemies."

"Anyone come to mind?" Kelly asked.

Josie thought for a moment. "I never have been a big fan of Matteo, Angela's husband, and she confided in me once that he had a bad temper and was very jealous that his wife was the number one winemaker in the valley. He said it was an embarrassment for an Italian man to have a wife who was better than he was."

"Does that possibly translate into a reason for murdering her?"

Josie shrugged. "Who knows? What I do find interesting is there is now a vacancy at the Moretti Winery for an experienced winemaker, and who better to fill the job than another winemaker who knows the grapes, the vineyards, and the operation? Kelly, that is sheer speculation, and I have nothing to base it on."

"All right, let's just say he could be a person of interest. Any others you can think of?"

Josie tipped her head to the side, and rolled a pen on her desk with her index finger. Foxie scampered back up onto her knee. "The wine industry here in the valley is pretty close, and it's often a rumor mill. I've heard it said several times that Carlos Romano of the Romano Winery, he's the one Matteo works for, was very jealous of the Moretti's success. From what I hear, he wants to be number one in the making of premium wines."

"So, since Matteo is working for him, Matteo could stay with him and make premium wines if another winemaker was hired by the Moretti Winery, or he could become the winemaker at the Moretti Winery. Interesting. Either way, it looks like he's going to have to make some decisions," Kelly said.

"Well, I hope that his decisions don't include Carlos Romano's niece, Alessandra. She's visiting her uncle for a year to learn about American winemaking, which would be fine, except gossip has it that she'd like to have more than a professional relationship with Matteo, and she's very beautiful."

Kelly's eyes narrowed. "Did Angela know about that? Maybe her death was the result of a crime of passion, say an argument between her and Matteo. Maybe she accused him of having an affair with the woman, although having an argument on the steps leading up to a wine vat is a bit of a stretch, I admit."

"I don't think Angela had heard about Alessandra. If she had, she never mentioned it to me. I don't know if Angela had ever seen her, but if she had, I would have thought she would have said something to me, because Alessandra could strike fear in the heart of any woman." Josie almost smiled for the first time that day.

"Why is that?"

"Let's put it this way. If Mike saw a gorgeous Italian woman with a lush body and she obviously had a thing for him, wouldn't that cause you some sleepless nights?"

"No question, and I hope he never sees her."

"My point exactly, but I agree with you. An argument on the steps leading up to the wine vat just wouldn't happen with two people in the wine industry. Wine is considered pretty sacred, and something like that would be beyond the scope of feasibility."

"Okay, given what you've told me, I think we could add both Carlos and his niece to the suspect list."

"I suppose. There's someone else who was jealous of Angela from what I've heard. Jim told me once that *Signora* Moretti had made some adverse comments about Angela."

"Really? That surprises me considering Angela was responsible for the superb wine produced here."

"From what I recall, it had nothing to do with wine," Josie went on. "Evidently *Signor* Moretti had a marital lapse many years ago, and *Signora* Moretti is a very jealous woman. Her comments to Jim were more about the fact her husband had to work with a woman as attractive as Angela. I guess she didn't like their close working relationship, but I never observed it being anything other than a professional relationship."

"Well, I suppose that's one more person to add to my list." Kelly tapped some notes into her cell phone. "Funny how you never think about these things until something like this happens. Anyone else?"

Josie appeared to be deep in thought for several long moments and then said, "There's an intern that was helping Angela. She's from the University of California at Davis. They have a very good wine program there, and one of the requirements is that their students who are working on their masters' degrees must intern at a winery for a one quarter during the school year. Caitlin Sanders is the name of the young woman who had been working as an intern for Angela."

"Why would she be a possible suspect?" Kelly asked, looking up from the screen on her phone.

"Only because I hear that she's very, very ambitious. She comes from a wealthy family and from what Angela told me, she's very intelligent, but feels that once she gets her master's degree, she should be able to get a job as a winemaker with any winery she decides she wants to work for. It makes sense to think that she'd want to work for the winery that produces the best wines in the valley, particularly after she's interned there. I think it's called 'a sense of entitlement.'"

"Well, that's a lot of food for thought." Kelly swiped her phone to off. "I'll run this by my husband and see what he thinks."

"I almost forgot to tell you, Kelly. The detective from the sheriff's office asked for the names of all the people who had been at the winery in the last month, and of course I gave him all of your names. I imagine he'll be in touch with you."

"Not a problem. Knowing my husband, he'll probably beat the sheriff's office to the punch and offer his services," Kelly said with a rueful smile. "Oh, and the reason my daughter isn't here to pick up the information about the wine is one of her children developed a high fever, so they went home to Calico Gold early this morning. She asked if I'd get it from you, but given everything that's happened, if you don't have it, don't worry about it."

Josie looked around the room. "Actually, I do have it somewhere. I got it yesterday after you left. I also have the cheese information for you. Let me get it," she said as she stood up and walked around her desk. "Here it is," she said as she reached down and picked up two manila folders that were on a side table. "I hope she can use it. She can mail it back to me whenever she's finished with it. I'm in no hurry."

Josie passed the folders over to Kelly. "Kelly, I'd love to talk to you longer, but I need to call the people who have scheduled wine tours for this week and cancel them per the sheriff's request. He doesn't want any new people on the premises for a couple of days. He said something about he thought it could muddy up things."

"I understand," Kelly said, rising to her feet. "Josie, one more question. What will happen to the wine in the vats? Isn't this kind of a critical time in the winemaking process?"

Josie's face turned somber once more. "Yes, *Signor* Moretti will need to make several decisions within a day or so. The wine that was in the vat where Angela was found will be destroyed, which is a huge loss to a small winery like this, but of course, there is no other option."

"Yes, I can see where that would have to be done." Kelly said as she walked towards the door, followed by Josie and Foxie. "Again, thanks for putting together the information for Julia and me, as well as for our conversation. If I can do anything to help you, please feel free to call me. You know where I'll be for the next two days." She touched Josie's arm. The petite blond's vulnerability touched her.

"Thanks for lending an ear, Kelly. I feel much better, but I think grief is beginning to settle in. Angela was a very dear friend, and I'm going to miss her more than you can imagine."

There was a knock on the door and Josie said, "Come in."

An attractive young woman walked in and said breathlessly, "Josie, what's happened. I drove into the parking lot, and there's yellow tape all over the place along with men and dogs. What's going on?"

"Caitlin, you better sit down. I have some terrible news. Angela died yesterday evening. Actually, the sheriff is treating it as a possible murder investigation."

The young woman stepped back, a stunned look on her face. "How can that be? She was fine yesterday when I was here. What happened?"

With Caitlin perched on the edge of the chair Kelly had just been sitting in, Josie told her everything she knew. While Caitlin was listening, Kelly was observing her from her vantage point in the doorway and noticed a strange look on her face. Kelly couldn't tell exactly what emotion she was experiencing, but it looked like something other than grief. It struck her as fear perhaps, or remorse.

"Oh, no. What a tragedy for the Moretti Winery," Caitlin exclaimed. "What will happen now?"

"I have no idea. Naturally, *Signor* Moretti was notified last night, but what he intends to do, I have no idea. I don't think there's anything for you to do this morning, so there's no reason for you to stay here. As far as the remainder of your time as an intern here, I just don't know right now."

Caitlin straightened up. "Well, of course things will have to be done to get the wine in the barrels and begin their aging. I'll come back tomorrow and see how I can help. I'm sure there are things that need to be done, and as you know, I've learned a lot from Angela. See you tomorrow," she said as she walked out of the room.

"Who was that?" Kelly asked. "She was quite something, if you don't mind me saying so."

"That's Caitlin Sanders. Sorry I didn't introduce you, but the conversation kind of got away from me. She's the intern I was telling you about from UC Davis. She's quite intelligent and someday will probably make a very good winemaker, but right now I think her elbows are a little too sharp for her age."

"What do you mean by that?" Kelly asked.

"Angela told me once that Caitlin felt she should be able to walk into any vineyard in the valley and immediately become their winemaker because of her brains and her educational studies. What she doesn't understood is that learning about the nuances of winemaking can't just come from a book. It must be experienced. She still has that to learn."

Kelly nodded sagely, noting that the clock on the wall indicated she'd been in Josie's office well over an hour. "Again, thanks for talking to me. I imagine my husband is getting close to finishing his golf game, so I better go. I'll be in touch," she said as she turned to leave.

Kelly walked out of Josie's office and over to where her car was parked, shuddering as she once again noticed the yellow tape surrounding the wine vat barn.

I wonder if Caitlin's ambitions had something to do with Angela's death. Stranger things have happened.

CHAPTER FIFTEEN

Kelly had just pulled into the bed and breakfast parking lot when her phone rang, and she could see from the name on the monitor that it was Mike.

Smiling, she took the call, leaving the engine running. "Well, Arnie, how did you do? Ready to be picked up?"

"I've had an amazing morning, Kelly. I actually shot the best golf game of my life. I can't believe it, and I even had two other men to play with. Best thing is, I even impressed them."

Kelly pictured Mike's beaming face. "You sound pretty pleased with yourself. Maybe it was the course. The Cedar Bay Public Golf Course probably doesn't hold a candle to the Sonoma Golf Club course."

"Yeah, you're probably right. After that phenomenal game, I'm starving. Let's have lunch after you pick me up."

"You're on." Kelly said as she put the car in drive. "Julia told me about a place on the square that she read had excellent lunches, and Sheriff, I've got a lot to tell you."

"Whenever you use that word it concerns me. Should I be concerned?" he asked.

"Not about thee, me, or any of our loved ones, but let's just say I've had a very interesting morning. See you in a few minutes."

"I'll be standing at the curb waiting with breathless anticipation to see what the latest thing is you've gotten us involved in," he said laughing, "and Kelly, it kind of boggles the mind to think we've been in this town for less than twenty-four hours, and you've already found something that I know will probably need my professional expertise."

"You got that right, love," she said before she hung up.

True to his word Mike was standing on the curb with a silly grin on his face. He stuck his thumb out when the car approached. As Kelly pulled to a stop, he opened the passenger door, then leaned over and gave her a kiss.

"What was that for?" she asked. "Mmmm. Maybe I should pick up hitchhikers more often."

"Let's just say you're the beneficiary of my fantastic morning." Mike said as he clicked his seat belt and then reached over and patted Kelly on the leg.

"Wow, you weren't kidding. You must have really shot a good game." Kelly put the car in gear and headed in the direction of the town square.

"It was better than that. The two men from Kansas I was playing with asked if I had been a pro when I'd been younger," he said, still grinning.

"And I assume you told them you had, but in your dotage you had a bucket list which included visiting the finest golf courses in the United States," she said, grinning back at him.

"Close, as the saying goes, but no cigar. I told them my bucket list included the best golf courses in the entire world, and I had just started to cross off the items after an early retirement."

"Mike, you didn't," she said as she took her eyes off the road to look at him and see if he was kidding.

"Kelly, watch the road." Mike leaned over and straightened the steering wheel. "No, I didn't say that, but it did cross my mind. I simply fessed up and told them the truth, that it was the best game I'd ever shot, and I have no idea why."

"Well, you could have crossed your fingers behind your back and told a little white lie. I used to do that, but I don't anymore."

"I know, Kelly, and believe me when I say I'm glad you decided to quit that dicey game of truth or dare."

"You knew I was doing that?" she asked incredulously, once again looking at him.

"The road, Kelly, eyes on the road. Yes, I knew, but I thought in the interests of a good marriage, it was best left unsaid."

She was quiet for a few moments and then said, "That was probably a wise decision."

"When do I get to hear about your morning?" he asked.

"When we're seated at the restaurant. It's right over there, and it even has an empty parking space in front of it. Must be our lucky day," she said as she parked in the space.

The hostess seated them and handed them menus. "In addition to what you see on the menu, the chef has created his signature muffin meat loaf as well as a dessert he serves every September. He calls it Gold Star Mother's Day Dessert. It's a red, white, and blue sweetened cream layered fruit sundae. People ask for it all year long, but he only serves it in September."

"I've never heard of Gold Star Mother's Day, and if it's that popular, why does he only serve it in September?" Kelly asked.

"The chef's brother was killed in action in Afghanistan a few years ago. The last Sunday in September is Gold Star Mother's Day which honors women whose sons or daughters died in combat. He honors both his brother and his mother with this dessert."

"That's one of the most touching things I've ever heard," Kelly said as she wiped a tear from her eye. It struck a chord with her since her son, Cash, was in a war zone on a tour of duty. "I'd like to look at the menu for a few minutes, but I know I definitely want that for dessert."

"Miss, you can make that two, and I'd like a chance to look at the menu, but I think you had me at the word meat loaf."

"Please, take your time. May I tell your waiter what you'd like to drink? This being Sonoma, we have a very good wine list."

"I'm sure you do, but a glass of iced tea with lemon sounds good to me," Kelly said.

"At the risk of being a parrot, you can make that two," Mike said as he opened his menu.

After a few minutes Kelly said, "I think I'm going to try the muffin meat loaf. That's probably something I could put on the menu at Kelly's Koffee Shop. Is that still your choice?"

"Actually, everything on the menu looks good, but yes, I've never had a muffin meat loaf before. Sounds interesting. Here comes our waiter with our iced tea. After he takes our orders, I want to hear about your morning, and please, don't leave out any relevant details."

CHAPTER SIXTEEN

Kelly spent the next half hour telling Mike about her conversation with Josie, stopping now and then to take another bite of her meat loaf, biscuit, mashed potatoes and green beans.

"Mike, I'm going to interrupt our conversation about Angela to find out what you think of these muffin meat loaves. Well?"

"They're excellent, and what a great idea for lunch. I really like the muffin idea. It's just like a regular meat loaf, but the muffin shape is unique and you don't overeat, because it's just the right size. You could even serve two muffin meat loaves, and then a customer could always take one home. It's a great idea."

"I've been seeing more and more things like these get on dinner menus. I think it has something to do with the cupcake craze. This is kind of an extension for people who like the concept, but want more than a sweet. It's something I'll definitely have to try when I get home, plus, although I rarely cater events, these would work just as well if they were made in mini-muffins pans and served as appetizers."

"Agreed, now back to Angela." Mike took the last bite of his meat loaf and started eyeing Kelly's. "I think we need go to the sheriff's office and save him the trouble of trying to find us. Plus, I can offer my services. We're kind of at loose ends, what with Julia and Brad gone, and quite frankly, doing wine tasting with them would have been fun because we'd get to spend time with them, but I'd be fine if we didn't do any more."

"So, if I'm hearing you correctly, we're about ready to get involved in trying to solve another murder mystery, or at least help, if we can." Kelly placed a protective arm around her plate and swatted Mike's arm away.

He was quiet for a few moments, and then he said, "Guess maybe that was the reason we had to come here. I kind of believe in signs…"

Kelly interrupted him, "You believe in signs? Since when? This is kind of new behavior for you. Are you going all woowoo on me? I thought you were strictly a by the rules kind of guy, not that I'm complaining, I'm just curious."

He smiled at her as he reached across the table and put his hand over hers. His touch sent a warm tingle up her arm. "Let's just say I've had a pretty good teacher the last few years."

"Thanks. That's something I never expected to hear from you, and I'll treasure it." After a busboy cleared their plates from the table, Kelly said, "I see that our dessert is on its way, and Mike, it's really beautiful."

The waiter placed the red white and blue desserts in front of each of them. "You'll see that the chef used the red and blue colors of the flag in his patriotic dish with raspberries, strawberries, and blueberries. The white is a mixture of melted white chocolate, mascarpone cheese, and whipped cream. Enjoy!"

They were both quiet for a few moments, enjoying the mixtures of flavors and feeling a bit patriotic. "Mike, this is definitely an I have to have the recipe for this dish if at all possible. Would you see if you can get the waiter's attention? I want to see if the chef will give me the recipe."

Mike scratched his cheek. "Kelly, is that really necessary? You do that everywhere we go. I think you could duplicate it quite easily."

Kelly wasn't taking no for an answer. "That may be true, but if the chef gives me the recipe I can use his name and give him some credit, and I'd like to do that. Anyone who comes up with something like this must be a pretty good guy."

When the waiter came over a few minutes later, Kelly said, "Would it be possible for me to get this dessert recipe from the chef? I really like it, and I'd like to feature it at the restaurant I own in Oregon. Of course I'd use the chef's name and give him credit."

"You're not the first to ask, ma'am, and the answer is yes. As a matter of fact, the chef made copies of it for use by his customers. His name is on the recipe. I'll be back in a minute with it for you."

"Thank you so much." Kelly winked at Mike. "See?" she smirked.

As soon as the waiter was out of earshot Mike leaned in and whispered, "Restaurant, Kelly? When did Kelly's Koffee Shop become a restaurant? Did I miss something?"

"Nope, it's sort of like the catch phrase 'you can catch more flies with honey than with vinegar'. Well, I've learned you get more people interested when you use the term restaurant rather than coffee shop."

"So, is this a way to get me to listen to what you say more carefully, so I won't be the victim of a smoke and mirrors trick?"

"Could be, Sheriff, could be. And speaking of sheriffs, let's ask the waiter where the sheriff's office is located when he returns, and then we'll be off on another adventure."

"Smoke and mirrors, Kelly." Mike pointed to something in the street, and when Kelly turned her head to look at it, his spoon pounced on her dessert. "Smoke and mirrors."

CHAPTER SEVENTEEN

They easily drove to the sheriff's station and parked in the area marked 'Visitors'. The station was about the size of Mike's, and from what Mike had found out when he'd done a quick search on the Internet, it serviced about the same number of people.

They walked up to the front desk, and Mike said to the young man sitting behind the desk, "My name is Sheriff Reynolds. I'm visiting here from Oregon and would like to see the sheriff about the murder of Angela Lucci. Would you please see if he's available to talk to me?"

"Of course, sir. Please have a seat over there," he said indicating a row of chairs against the wall. Kelly and Mike walked over and sat down in the sparsely furnished waiting room. Even the freshly painted walls couldn't disguise its drabness.

They could see the young man talking on the phone and less than a minute later a man who could have passed for Mike's twin opened a door and walked towards them. He was a large man with short salt and pepper hair, a slight paunch, and he carried an air of authority about him as he crossed the distance to where they were sitting. "Sheriff Reynolds, I'm Sheriff Dawson," he said as he held out his hand.

Mike showed the sheriff his identification and shook his hand. He turned towards Kelly, "Sheriff, this is my wife, Kelly Reynolds. We're visitors here in Sonoma enjoying a short vacation."

"Glad to have you. We can use all the tourist money we can get," he said laughing. "Please, come back to my office. You saved my deputies the trouble of trying to find you."

When they got to his office he sat behind his desk and indicated for them to sit in the chairs across from it. "Again, thanks for coming in. I understand from Josie that you were among the last people to see Angela Lucci before she was found dead. I understand she came into the tasting room briefly and spoke with you on her way to see the manager. What can you tell me about that?"

"Nothing, really. She came in, talked to us for a few minutes, and then left. If she hadn't died, I never would have given the meeting a second thought," Mike answered, placing an elbow on his knee.

"Sheriff, you know the drill, but humor me, I need to ask some questions. Naturally, we're in the very early stages of the investigation so whatever you can tell me might save us some time."

"Of course, Sheriff, we're happy to help you however we can."

"Did you notice anything strange about Angela? Did she seem distraught, nervous, or anxious? Being a sheriff, did you get a sense that something was off? Mrs. Reynolds, I've found that women are often more tuned to the nuances of moods than men are. Did you get any vibes from your meeting with the decedent?"

They both answered in the negative. "Sheriff, I wish we could help you with that, but there was nothing unusual about our conversation with her. She was very calm and likeable. She was one of those people who seemed to be very much at home in her own skin, if you know what I mean," Mike said.

"I do, and the others we've talked to who saw her yesterday have said pretty much the same thing. Her husband seemed very distraught when he heard the news, but that's not unusual."

"We never met him. Sheriff, this is going to sound kind of strange, but my wife has been very helpful to me in solving some murders that have occurred in my jurisdiction. Actually, she's also helped solve murders in Calico Gold, Italy, and Cuba. We came here to meet our daughter and son-in-law and do some wine-tasting. Our daughter is a wine scholar and teaches education classes on wine. Unfortunately, one of their children developed a high fever last night, and they left Sonoma to go back home early this morning, so we're kind of at loose ends."

"Is that a roundabout way of telling me that you'd be willing to help me solve this case?" Sheriff Dawson asked.

"Well, we're here, and we've had quite a bit of experience doing this type of thing. I sure don't want to step on anyone's toes, particularly yours, but if you'd like us to, we could nose around and see what we might be able to find out," Mike said.

The sheriff looked directly at Kelly. "Mrs. Reynolds, I'm curious. Do you have a background in law enforcement?"

"I think I can answer that, Sheriff," Mike said. "My wife has a way with people. They trust her and often tell her things they wouldn't tell other people. That's not say it hasn't led to some situations that have been pretty dicey. As a matter of fact, she's licensed to carry a gun, and she has a guard dog with her pretty much all the time when she finds herself involved in a criminal investigation. The guard dog and the gun are with her at my request."

"That's one of the more provocative statements I've ever heard," Sheriff Dawson said. "Did you bring your guard dog and gun with you to Sonoma?"

"No, we flew to Sacramento, rented a car, and drove over here to Sonoma. It never occurred to me I'd need either one, but I kind of wish I had both of them right now," Mike said.

"I'm sure you do. That's the down side of flying. Registering a gun is a pain in the neck which, believe me, I know from personal experience. Okay, Mrs. Reynolds, what's your take on the death of Angela Lucci? Have you found out anything?"

"Actually, she has," Mike said, "although you may already know about these, for lack of a better word, persons of interest. Kelly, why don't you tell the sheriff about your morning?"

Kelly told him about her conversation with Josie and ended a half hour later by saying, "I hope I didn't bore you by duplicating what you've probably already found out. If I've said anything that helps, I'm glad I was able to be of assistance. I know Mike always says that nothing is insignificant when you're trying to solve a murder mystery."

Sheriff Dawson laughed and turned towards Mike. "Sheriff, you have to be the luckiest man in the world."

"I think I am, but what makes you say that?"

"I spent most of last night with Josie, Jim, and my deputies. Other than the obvious husband, not one person of interest was mentioned. Your wife has found out more in a morning than I could have in several days. You've just saved me and my deputies a lot of time and work. At least we have places to start when we finish our preliminary work."

"What do you consider the preliminary work, if I might ask?" Kelly said.

"Right now my people are searching the entire vineyard for any clues that might help. Angela's office is being searched, and one of our computer experts is going over her computer. We want to find out who she talked to and what she did in the days leading up to her death. I want to get a statement from her doctor, so we can rule out a heart attack or some other health issue that might not make this a case of murder, although we are treating it as one at this time. She was young and from what people have said, including her husband, she didn't appear to have any health issues."

"Since your hands are going to be full sifting through what your deputies find, it might help if Kelly and I see what we can find out about the persons of interest. No one knows us in the area, and we might be able to find out more than someone associated with the sheriff's department could."

Sheriff Dawson was quiet for a few moments and then said, "I think that's an excellent idea, and I can't thank both of you enough for volunteering to spend your vacation helping my department. Just sit here for a moment, and I'll be right back," he said as he walked out the door, closing it softly behind him.

"What do you think he's doing?" Kelly asked.

"I have no idea."

The door opened a few minutes later and the sheriff returned. "Sheriff Reynolds, I'm assuming that if your wife didn't want to take the time to register a gun with the airlines, you didn't either. Here's a gun for each of you. They're registered to me, so they won't be a problem. Try not to use them, but we all know there are times when it's necessary."

"That's very generous of you, Sheriff, considering you really don't know us," Mike said.

"Matter of fact I feel like I do. When Tyler called to tell me you were here, I told him to call the head of the California State Sheriff's Association and see what he could find out about you. Evidently he knows people in Oregon and when I went to get your guns, Tyler gave me the report. You've got an excellent reputation in law enforcement."

"If I hadn't, would you have given us the guns?" Mike asked smiling.

"Nope, not when my name's attached to these weapons."

"Sheriff, I'm sure you probably collected lots of DNA material, fingerprints, and anything else you thought might be relevant. Any clues or information you can share with us? Obviously, it won't go any farther."

"We got two sets of shoe prints on the steps leading up to the top of the wine vat. We assume that one set belongs to the decedent, but there's a good chance that the other set is the murderer's. That's why I'm tentatively treating this case as a murder. From what Jim and Josie told us, there is no reason for a second set of shoe prints to be on the stairs. For the last few days, no one has been up and down the stairs except Angela Lucci."

"When you find out more about that, would you give me a call? That could be really important," Mike said.

"Yes. I expect to have something on it this evening. My deputies have impounded all of Angela's shoes, including the ones she was wearing, as evidence and they're checking the sole prints now. I'll let you know. Here's a pen and a piece of paper." He pushed them across the table. "Would you write down where you're staying as well as your cell phone numbers in case I need to get in touch with you? Is there anything else you can think of?"

Mike started to get up, but Kelly put her hand out, restraining him. "Sheriff, I know this is kind of out of the box, but…"

"Kelly, it seems like you've told the sheriff everything, and I'm sure he has other things to do to get this case moving," Mike said.

"No, Mike, I want to hear what Kelly has to say. It sounds like she has very good instincts regarding things. What did you want to say?"

"Well, I told you about the dog, Foxie, barking, and that's what alerted Josie that something was wrong. I'm sure she told you the same thing."

"Yes, she did."

"From what I understand, Angela always left the door to the vat barn slightly ajar so Foxie could see her. That means that while Foxie couldn't actually get into the vat barn, she would have seen the murderer enter the barn. I seem to remember Josie telling me that was the only way in and out of the barn."

"If I'm hearing you correctly, you're saying that Foxie could recognize the murderer. Is that right?"

"That's right, but I'm not sure how she can help you. Even if she could identify the murderer, I don't think it would hold up in a courtroom. Would that be correct?"

"Yes, that's true," Mike said, "but what's interesting is that if the murderer was identified that way, it sure would eliminate a lot of other people. It's an interesting concept, but I have no idea how we would be able to implement it."

"Nor do I," Sheriff Dawson said. "I need to think about that. Thanks, Kelly. I'll be in touch as soon as we find out about the shoe prints, and if you come across anything, I'd appreciate you giving me a call. Here's my card, and I've written my cell phone number on the back. Again, thank you both for coming in. I know it would have been a lot easier to shop and wine-taste rather than work on solving a possible murder. Glad there are still people like you two around."

He walked around his desk and shook both of their hands and then opened the door.

After they got in their car, Kelly said, "Mike, what did you think of him?"

"I liked him, and I feel sorry for him. I've been in that predicament where you'd really like to spend your time going after the person you consider to be of interest, but you can't start with them until you've done all your due diligence or some sharp lawyer will tear your case to shreds when it goes to court. I just hope we can help."

"We will. What do you think we should do next?"

"I'd like to go out to the winery and talk to the manager of the Moretti Winery and vineyards. He might have thought of something, and he probably knows as much about what goes on there as anyone."

"Good idea. Glad the sheriff said we could use his name. That might give you some credibility with him."

CHAPTER EIGHTEEN

When Kelly and Mike arrived at the Moretti Winery, a number of law enforcement personnel were just finishing up their investigation. Mike walked over to the man who seemed to be in charge and introduced himself.

"Hi, I'm Sheriff Reynolds visiting here from Oregon," Mike said as he showed the deputy sheriff his identification. "I just spent some time with Sheriff Dawson, and I'll be lending a hand with the investigation while I'm here. Find anything of interest?"

"Nothing that would point to who did it, assuming she didn't just accidentally fall in the wine vat. From talking to the manager and the tour guide, both of whom seemed to know her well, she was far too careful to let something like that happen. I think it's a pretty safe assumption she was pushed in. Wish I had more to tell you and Sheriff Dawson. Maybe we'll get lucky with some of the prints."

"Well, good luck. This won't be easy. I heard there weren't any signs of trauma on the body when she was pulled out of the vat."

"That's correct, sir, which is another reason we believe she was pushed into the vat. The coroner is doing an autopsy on her to see if she was poisoned or if she had some medical issue that caused her to fall in the vat, possibly a stroke or a heart attack."

"I'm assuming you've talked to her husband about any health issues she might have had. How is he doing?"

"He's in shock. He says his wife was in excellent health, and that just corroborates our thoughts that this wasn't an accident. He said he planned on spending the next few hours calling family members in Italy. He said his wife had made so many friends in the valley that he thought he should hold the funeral here, rather in Italy. He also said he thought her family would probably hold some type of memorial service for her at their village church. It's a sad situation."

"I agree. Thanks for taking the time to talk to me."

Kelly and Mike walked up the steps to where the winery offices and tasting room were located. Kelly turned and paused for a second. "Mike, why don't you go talk to Jim? I want to see how Josie is doing."

"Sure. Let's meet here on the porch when we're finished. I don't think it will take too long," he said as he opened the door. "As I recall from yesterday, Josie said the manager's office was down this hall."

Kelly retraced her earlier footsteps and knocked on Josie's door. In response to "Who is it?" she answered, "Josie, it's me, Kelly Reynolds. My husband is helping Sheriff Dawson, and he wanted to talk with Jim, so I came with him. I thought I'd pop by and see how you are doing."

When she entered, she saw Josie sitting at her desk and noticed how pale she was. "Come on in, Kelly. In answer to your question, I'm doing okay. It's hard when your best friend has died and was probably murdered. I kind of feel like I can't trust anyone, and that's a new feeling for me."

"I can well imagine. I see that Foxie has bonded with you," Kelly said, referring to the dog that was fast asleep on Josie's lap.

"Yeah, poor little girl. She and Angela were very close. Angela took her everywhere she went, even put her in the car when she had to go into town. I'm glad she's accepting me. I can't imagine anything worse than seeing someone you love murdered."

"From that statement, I take it that you've had time to think about it, and you're pretty sure Angela was murdered."

Josie's eyes met Kelly's. "No, I'm not pretty sure. I am absolutely certain. Angela was a stickler for safety. When she came to work here, she borrowed a handyman from Jim. He does all kinds of repair things around here, from fixing a sagging fence to repairing a broken water main. He's really a jack-of-all trades. Anyway, she had him do some research to find out what could be applied to the steps leading up to the top of the vats that would provide a rough surface, so she wouldn't slip. Angela was that kind of a person. Nothing was too small to escape her attention if it involved safety. No, there is absolutely no way she would have slipped and fallen into the vat."

Kelly sat down and took some peppermints from her purse. Opening the pack, she offered one to Josie. "I understand the coroner is going to do an autopsy and some tests to see if Angela had a medical problem that could have caused her to fall. I guess he's also going to see if there were any foreign substances in her body as well."

"In my opinion that's an utter waste of his time," Josie said, sucking on the candy. "She had her annual checkup with her doctor last week, and I remember her telling me that the doctor said if all his patients were in as good as health she was in, he wouldn't have a job." She shook her head from side to side. "No, Angela did not have a medical problem."

"What about foreign substances, such as drugs or alcohol?" Kelly asked.

Josie thought it over. "Once in a while she and I would share a glass of wine late in the day after my last wine tour, but we didn't yesterday. On the infrequent occasions when we did that, the most wine she ever had was one glass. She limited her wine consumption because she said her palate needed to be sharp for her tasting of the wine in the vats or what she did on a revolving basis with the wines in the barrels."

"I see. She must have had an incredible ability to differentiate tastes."

"Angela had the most sophisticated palate of any wine person I've ever known. I would taste a wine and say it was fine, and I've had a lot of training. Not Angela. She would taste the same wine and throw away the bottle because to her taste, there was a hint of something off. I mean, no one who bought the wine would ever be able to taste it, but Angela could. It was pretty amazing."

"I would think she'd at least give the bottle to someone who probably couldn't afford to buy it."

"No. Anything that came from this winery had to pass her exacting standards, and trust me, they were the most stringent I've seen in the wine industry. She was very clear that only the best wines would be available at the Moretti Winery and anything that was less was to be disposed of, and not by drinking it."

Kelly raised an eyebrow. "I'm sure a lot of owners wouldn't have been all that happy with her philosophy. I'm guessing *Signor* Moretti was."

"Yes, he agreed completely. In his own way, he's just as careful that this winery produces only the best wines. As a matter of fact, he called a little while ago and told me he was coming here to talk to Matteo about taking over Angela's job."

"Isn't that a little soon? Poor guy's not going to have much time to grieve."

"That's true. Angela told me once that there's a saying in Italy that pasta waits for no man. She said that it should have been wine waits for no man, and there is some truth in that statement. Timing is everything in wine production, and even if there's been a murder, the winemaking process must continue. Matteo is well aware of it."

"Two things, Josie, and then I won't take up any more of your time. How do you feel about Matteo getting the job and secondly, you never answered my question about Angela and foreign substances?"

Josie's face became stern. "Let me start with the foreign substances, because that's so cut and dried it requires only a couple of words. Angela did not ever do drugs. That's the answer, and I repeat, ever. As a matter of fact, she once laughed that she'd never even tried marijuana, and it was on her bucket list before she died."

"Okay, what about her relationship with Matteo? Maybe I should ask if there was another man in her life. She was quite attractive."

Josie looked away and was silent for a while before continuing. "Emphatically, there was no one else in her life, but Matteo. Angela adored him and in his own way, I think he adored her. As I mentioned this morning, he was jealous of her. Having him take over her position is going to be hard for me, but if he has the good of the winery at heart, then I'm sure it will work out. I'll just feel a whole lot better about it when the murderer is found, and it's not Matteo. I know he's hurting, because he was crying when I called a little while ago to tell him *Signor* Moretti would be here later and wanted to talk to him."

"Is he at home now?"

"He was when I called, and I haven't seen his truck leave, so I'm assuming he is. Why?"

"I'd like to talk to him and offer my condolences," Kelly said, putting the peppermints back in her purse. "I think you mentioned yesterday that his house is the one on the end. Right?"

"Yes."

"Thanks. I'm going to head up there. See you later," Kelly said as she left Josie's office and walked towards Matteo's house.

CHAPTER NINETEEN

Kelly knocked on the door of the attractive red-tiled house with the cream-colored siding and pots of fall plants blooming in a riot of color on the steps and the porch. She wasn't too surprised that it was neat and attractive, given what she'd heard about Angela.

The door was opened by one of the handsomest men Kelly had ever seen. Her immediate thought was, *If I were twenty years younger...*

The man standing in front of her had jet-black hair pulled back into a ponytail, soft brown eyes that looked like they'd recently been wet with tears, a smooth olive complexion, and was wearing a white tee shirt over jeans, which accentuated his muscular body.

"Yes, may I help you?" he asked.

"My name is Kelly Reynolds. I was on a tour here yesterday and briefly met your wife. I want to express my condolences."

"Thank you, please come in. I just got off the phone with relatives in Italy. It is not a happy day."

Kelly followed him inside. The small house was decorated in white throughout with a vibrant assortment of colorful accessories bringing the place to life. A hand painted vase containing cut wildflowers and a watercolor of the ocean next to a stack of old books clearly indicated a woman's touch and a simple life lived well.

"I can only imagine. Matteo, I know this is rather indelicate, but the sheriff's department is treating Angela's death as if the cause was possibly murder. My husband is a sheriff in Oregon, and we're here for a short time. Due to some unforeseen circumstances, the people we were meeting here had to leave unexpectedly. When we found out about Angela's death, my husband offered to help the sheriff. He's talking to Jim, the winery manager, right now. I was wondering if you have anything to add to what you've already told the sheriff."

"Please sit down and forgive me for what the house looks like. Angela was a very exacting housekeeper, me not so much." He stopped talking and looked down at his hands which were tightly clenched.

Kelly moved some papers from the couch and sank back into its softness.

Matteo remained standing, nervously pacing back and forth. He hesitated for a moment and then said, "I didn't tell the sheriff or his deputy about something that happened yesterday between Angela and me, because I was afraid they would think I murdered her."

"Why would they think that?" Kelly asked.

"Because I was very abrupt with Angela yesterday morning. I had what I guess you Americans would call a temper tantrum, and I became very angry with her. We'd had arguments and discussions about her being the winemaker here many times. After we had the argument yesterday, I stormed out. I knew what the sheriff would think, and I probably would have thought the same thing, but it wasn't that way."

It was easy to see that Matteo was grieving deeply and trying not to fall apart in front of her. He took a long, deep breath before continuing.

"I loved Angela more than anything in the world, but sometimes I just got angry about the winemaking. It's kind of hard when your wife is more successful than you are, at least it was for me. It's all my fault she died. You see, I often went with her to the vat barn. She'd take Foxie, and I'd go in the barn with her. It was an unwritten agreement that I wouldn't interfere when she was tasting the wine, so I usually checked my email messages while she did her tastings."

"Why didn't you go with her last night?" Kelly asked.

"I was in town, buying a bouquet of flowers for her at the florist's. After the way I'd acted yesterday morning, I knew I needed to do something special for her. I wanted it to be unique, so I asked the florist to make a bouquet that was like the one she carried down the aisle when we got married. She was so beautiful in that dress..." He started sobbing and put his head in his hands.

I'm a pretty good judge of character, and I have one of the strongest feelings I've ever had that Matteo had nothing to do with Angela's death, Kelly thought.

Kelly stood up and walked over to him, laying her hand on his shoulder. "Matteo, if she was in fact murdered, I know there's nothing I can do to make your pain go away, but I want you to know that I will do everything I can to make sure that the murderer is found and you're no longer a suspect."

Matteo raised his hands in frustration. "What could you possibly do? This is an impossible situation. When you knocked on the door, I was sure it was the sheriff who had come to arrest me. You must believe me. I had nothing to do with Angela's death, and I certainly didn't murder her."

"Right now, I don't know exactly what I can do, but I'm certain there is something. I told you my husband's a sheriff. What I didn't tell you is that I've helped him solve a number of murders in the past. I don't know why, but I seem to have a knack for it. I understand that *Signor* Moretti is coming to talk to you in a little while. If you don't mind, I'd like to ask you some questions, so I can get started."

"Why are you doing this for me?" he asked, lifting his head from his hands.

"I have a son who is away from home. Actually, he's on a military tour of duty in Afghanistan. If he was ever accused of something, I would hope someone would help him. Other than that, I have no rational answer, it's just something I feel I need to do."

"Thank you. I could tell when I talked to Angela's parents, that although they didn't say anything, they obviously wondered how I could allow this to happen or worse. Yes, perhaps they thought I was the murderer. You see, in Italy, we protect our women. I obviously didn't. Not only is Angela dead, I've spoiled the Lucci name," he said as tears again filled his eyes.

"Matteo, you can't go back. What's done is done, but I think Angela would want more than anything for your name to be cleared, so let's begin. You mentioned you were at a florist's yesterday evening. Can you tell me when you were there and who helped you?"

"Yes, I was at Paula's Posies. It's the florist that's on the square in town. I know the name is kind of silly, but Paula told me once she gave her shop that name because it was easy to remember. Angela loved flowers, so I often bought bouquets for her. Paula was the one who helped me. I was there from about 6:30 to 7:30."

"That seems like an awfully long time to pick out a bouquet."

"It was. She even had to stay late because of me, but I've been a good customer. Like I told you, I was trying to do something really special and that was to try and duplicate all the flowers that were in her bridal bouquet the day we were married."

"And were you able to?" Kelly asked.

"Yes, but it wasn't easy. In fact, Paula did quite a big favor for me. She had previously made up several floral arrangements she was going to deliver today, but some of the flowers I wanted were only in those bouquets, so she had to take several apart. She said she would have one of the flower growers make a special delivery to her this morning to fill them back in."

"This has no relevance, Matteo, so forgive me, but my feminine curiosity would like to know what flowers Angela carried on her wedding day."

"It was a beautiful bouquet of white baby orchids, the palest pink baby roses, white freesias, and pale orchid roses. She had baby's breath and ferns in it as well. It turned out just like when we were married."

Kelly had noticed the wedding photo of them on the fireplace mantle, a radiant Angela holding a bouquet exactly like the one Matteo had described. "So, you were with Paula that whole time? Is that correct?"

"Yes. I got there about 6:30 and left her shop about 7:30. From Paula's shop, I went to the chocolatier in town and bought a box of chocolate truffles, because they were Angela's favorite."

"Who waited on you?"

"The owner, Salvatore DeMarco. Since he's from Italy, we've developed kind of a friendship, plus I go there every few months to buy truffles for Angela. He was the one who sold them to me last night."

"How long were you there?"

"Probably fifteen minutes. We talked a little of this and that, nothing really important. He giftwrapped the truffles in a box and put a special bow on it. One of his helpers even admired it, so she can vouch for me as well."

"That covers the time from 6:30 to about 8:00. Would that be correct?"

"Yes, as a matter of fact I looked at the clock in my truck when I pulled into the winery, and it was a few minutes after eight. I couldn't figure out what was happening because there were so many red and blue flashing lights. I realized something had happened, but I never…" He stopped and took a deep breath. "I never thought for a minute the lights and the people were there because my wife had been found dead in one of the wine vats. It was surreal."

"What happened then?" Kelly asked.

It took Matteo a few long moments to compose himself, and then he said in a shaky voice, "I got out of my truck, and the sheriff came over to me. He was the one who told me Angela was dead…" He stopped talking and looked out the window into the distance, tears coursing down his cheeks.

Matteo continued, "I guess he'd been told I was driving my truck and he was waiting for me to return. He was very nice, and said he knew it wasn't a good time to talk to me, but at some point, he would need to take a statement from me. He told one of his men to accompany me to my house. Josie and Jim were there along with Foxie. Josie told me about how she'd found Angela. She offered to keep Foxie for a few days, so I wouldn't have to care for her."

"I can only imagine what you must have been going through," Kelly said.

"No, I don't think you can. However bad you may think it was, multiply it by a hundred or a thousand times. I think in some ways I'm still in shock. I can't believe my Angela is dead…"

They both were quiet for several minutes, and then Kelly said, "I assume you had to call some people, like your boss, to tell him you wouldn't be at work today."

A dark and angry look crossed over Matteo's face. Kelly looked closely at him and said, "Matteo, what was that look about?" She saw the wild fury in his eyes.

"Nothing, it is nothing," he said with an angry edge in his voice.

Kelly stood her ground. "Matteo, the only thing I know for sure when it comes to investigating a murder case, is that everything could be important, no matter how small or insignificant it can seem to you. Please, tell me what you're thinking."

"I'm sure it is nothing. Carlos Romano, my boss, and I were talking yesterday and..."

After he told Kelly about the conversation he was quiet for several moments, then he continued, "Carlos has always been very good to me. We both wanted his wines to be the best in the valley, but we couldn't make it happen. I think his references to Angela and the possibility of her falling in one of the wine vats was just a form of frustration. There is nothing I know about him that would make me think he is capable of committing murder, plus everyone knows him. He couldn't walk into this winery without being recognized. I'm sure it was nothing."

Kelly thought about the words Carlos had used which Matteo had just described to her. The detail Carlos had gone into about how Angela might die unnerved her. "I'm sure you're right, but I'll run it by my husband. Let me ask you something since you've brought his name up. Do you think *Signor* Romano could have had anything to do with Angela's death?"

"No, I don't think so. Carlos is a very honorable man." He shrugged his shoulders. "Kelly, every winery owner in the valley wants his wines to be the best. Carlos was no different. I think his words yesterday were just an expression of his frustration, nothing more..."

He was interrupted by the ringing of his cell phone. "Excuse me," he said to Kelly. He turned away and took the phone out of his back pocket. "This is Matteo." He listened for a moment and then said, "Yes. Please tell Jim and *Signor* Moretti I will be there in a few moments." He turned to Kelly. "I must leave. *Signor* Moretti is here, and he wants to talk to me."

"One last question, Matteo. If he offers you the job of winemaker here, will you take it?"

"It has been a dream of mine since *Signor* Moretti asked Angela and me to come to California. Yes, I will, even though the dream has turned into a nightmare. Excuse me, I need to get my shoes."

A moment later he returned wearing a pair of sandals with Velcro fasteners and rubber soles. Kelly looked down at his feet and said, "Those seem like a very strange type of shoe to wear in a vineyard."

"Actually, most of the people who are in and out of the winery buildings and the vineyards wear them. It's so much easier than unlacing shoes every time you come into a building because of the mud we get on them. This way we can take them off and most of us keep a pair of slip-ons handy, so we can change quickly."

"I've never heard of that, but it makes sense."

"It makes so much sense there's a shoe store just off the plaza that caters to wine people. Everyone in the industry buys their shoes from them." Together, Matteo and Kelly walked out of his house and headed towards the building where Jim's office was located.

"Matteo, what about your job with *Signor* Romano?" Kelly asked.

He smiled sardonically. "I imagine his niece, Alessandra, will stay here and take over my job, which means I'll have to see her a lot more than I'd like to."

"What do you mean by that?"

"Alessandra is a very beautiful Italian woman who has made it very clear that I could be the object of her affections. Now that I no longer have a wife," he said with a catch in his voice, "I imagine she will make herself very available to me. I was looking forward to her return to Italy, because not only is she interested in me, but a woman who looks like her could be trouble."

As they walked up the steps to the building, Kelly said, "Matteo, here's my card with my cell phone number on it. I doubt if there is much I can do to help, but if you think of something, please let me know."

"I will, and thanks for listening to me."

"I only wish it could have been under more pleasant circumstances, but I do plan on talking to the people who can attest to the fact that you were at the flower and chocolate shops at the time of your wife's death. If she was murdered, that doesn't tell us who the murderer is, but it should clear your name."

"Thank you," he said simply, as he opened the door to the building.

CHAPTER TWENTY

Mike knocked on the door with the words, "Jim Barstow, Manager," on it and immediately heard a voice say, "Come in."

He walked into the spacious office which had a large window on the far side overlooking the vineyards. "Hi. My name is Sheriff Mike Reynolds. My wife and I came to Sonoma for a little vacation with her daughter and son-in-law, but they had to leave unexpectedly when one of their children became ill. My wife was here earlier getting some information from Josie and found out about the death of your winemaker, Angela. Apparently the sheriff thinks her death involves some suspicious circumstances, and he's investigating her death as a possible murder. I talked to Sheriff Dawson and volunteered my services to help him solve the crime. He's pretty busy at the moment, so I thought I might be able to help."

Jim greeted Mike with a handshake. "You can probably do a lot more than that, Sheriff. I just heard on the news that there's been a terrible seven-car accident on the main highway leading into Sonoma, and five people are dead with six others in critical condition. I think the sheriff has his hands full. Like it or not, it looks like right now you're probably the lead investigator in this case."

"I didn't count on that," Mike said, "but if I can help, I know I'd appreciate it if someone did the same for me."

"What can I do for you? I can't talk to you for very long because *Signor* Moretti is coming here to talk to Matteo about taking over Angela's job. It's an awkward time, but the business of making wine must go on."

"I'd like your opinion of Matteo Lucci, Carlos Romano, and *Signor* and *Signora* Moretti. I haven't met any of them, but from the brief amount I've been told, they are all persons who could be of interest in this case, and from what you've just told me, I rather doubt that Sheriff Dawson will get around to talking to them anytime soon."

Jim motioned for Mike to sit at the small table by the window. Joining him, Jim put his hand under his chin and thought for several moments. The breathtaking vista of the vineyards beyond the parking lot below provided a glorious technicolor backdrop to the discussion that followed.

"Let's take them one by one, Sheriff," Jim began. "I'll start with Matteo. He's a very handsome, hot-blooded Italian man, and if it hadn't been for his wife, I'm sure *Signor* Moretti would have hired him. His wine knowledge and palate are that good. Unfortunately, his wife's was a just a little bit better. If he accepts the job here, he will do fine."

"You say he's hot-blooded. What do you mean by that?"

"He has a quick temper, but I've never seen him become physical. Angela mentioned one time that they often argued in the Italian way with loud words and anger, followed by some wonderful making up times. I always gathered it was a cultural thing. From everything I know of him, he was a devoted husband. I heard talk from time to time about him with this woman or that woman, but I have no direct knowledge of him ever being unfaithful to Angela."

"Have you heard anything recently?"

"Yes, but I'm sure it was nothing. Even though the wineries are in competition with one another, there is still a sense of camaraderie among the workers, and particularly the winery managers. The manager at Carlos Romano's winery and I went to school together, and we get together almost weekly for a glass of wine and just to talk."

"Your employers don't mind?"

"No, they get together too. Anyway, the last time my friend and I were talking, he mentioned that he'd be glad when Carlos Romano's niece, Alessandra, returned to Italy because although she'd been very quick to learn the way wine is made here in the valley, every time Matteo was around the only thing she could do was stare at him, and he said it wasn't with sisterly looks."

"What did you make of that?"

"Not much. Often the blood runs hot in young people, and Alessandra is a very attractive woman, but so was Angela, so I never saw it as a problem. As a matter of fact, my friend said that Matteo would be a fool to jeopardize his marriage to a woman like Angela, and I agreed."

"All right, what about the Morettis?"

"I like *Signor* Moretti a lot. The *Signora*, just between you and me, not so much. It's rumored that he married her for her money. Evidently her family in Italy is very wealthy, although his family does quiet well with the winery they own and operate. She's beautiful, but she's a little sharp for my taste. She seems to frown a lot, which I know seems petty, but that's my impression of her. I don't think she's happy."

"Do you have any idea why?" Mike asked.

Jim paused and looked down at his hands. "I really don't like to say anything negative about my employers."

"I understand that, but it may be important. A woman was possibly murdered here at the winery, so anything you tell me could be very important."

Jim sighed and then said, "One time when they were getting ready to leave the winery, they got in their car and the windows were down. They were talking in loud voices. I wasn't eavesdropping, I just couldn't avoid hearing them. Their car was in the parking lot right below my window, which was open.

"It had to do with Angela. *Signora* Moretti was very angry about the amount of time her husband spent with Angela. She said something to the effect she was sure it would end up in an affair like the one he'd had several years ago. She said she would not go through that again and would rather see Angela dead than have that happen."

"Wow. I can see why you didn't want to tell me that. What did he say?"

"He told her that he had to spend a lot of time with his winemaker. He said that's why their wines were the best, because everyone here worked as a team, from the manager, meaning me, to the seasonal help in the vineyards. He assured her he wasn't having an affair and said he learned his lesson many years ago."

"What happened then?"

"He started the car, and they left. That was the only time I ever heard words between them, but *Signor* Moretti usually comes here by himself. Whether that's because *Signora* Moretti doesn't want to see Angela or for some other reason, or maybe none, I don't know."

"What about Carlos Romano?"

"I don't know much about him other than what my friend tells me. I've never heard anything negative about him or his winery. Sure, there's some envy on his part. Like I said earlier, everyone here in the valley wants to have the best wine, and when you're the one who comes in second every year, that has to be frustrating."

"You mentioned his niece, Alessandra. Anything about her other than what you've told me?"

"No, not a thing. I understand she's scheduled to go back to Italy in a few months, but with all of this, who knows?"

They heard a car engine and Jim looked out his window. "That's *Signor* Moretti. Since you're representing Sheriff Dawson and you want to meet him, you might as well stay here and talk to him before our meeting with Matteo."

He stood up, walked over to the door, and opened it. A moment later a large silver-haired man walked into the room. "*Signor*, it's good to see you. Let me introduce you to Sheriff Reynolds. He's helping Sheriff Dawson with the investigation into Angela's death. Sheriff Reynolds, I'd like you to meet the owner of the winery, Giovanni Moretti."

"Sheriff, it's nice to meet you, and please call me Gio," he said, his forthright gaze sizing up Mike. "Thank you for any help you may be able to provide in connection with Angela's death. I just heard there was a horrible crash out on Highway 12. I imagine Sheriff Dawson's on overload about now."

"You're probably right. I'd like to express my condolences on the death of your winemaker, Angela. Of course, we don't know for sure that she was murdered, but it's starting to look that way. Since Sheriff Dawson is going to be tied up with the traffic accident investigation, I'll do everything I can for the next couple of days to help."

"We appreciate it. Sheriff, is there anything you need from me?"

"Not really. I am curious how you happened to hire Angela. I don't think I've heard that."

Gio crossed his legs and relaxed back in his chair. "Angela and Matteo both worked at my family's winery in Tuscany. For many years I have had a successful winery in the Napa region, and I wanted to try my hand at a boutique winery and concentrate on producing a top quality wine. This winery here in Sonoma became available on the market, so I went to my family to ask their opinion. They felt I should buy it and have Angela as my winemaker. They had worked with Angela and Matteo for several years in Italy and felt she was just a little more knowledgeable and her palate was just a little better."

"*Signor*, is it unusual for a woman to be a winemaker?" Mike asked.

"While it's not unusual, they are definitely in the minority, both here and in Italy. When Angela and Matteo came to live here in Sonoma, she became like a daughter to me. I have two sons who work with me at the winery in Napa, but she was like the daughter I never had, and I loved her as a daughter." His eyes became shiny with tears, and he raised a hand to his eyes, dropping his head for a moment as he struggled to regain his composure.

After a few moments, he resumed speaking. "Please, I beg of you, Sheriff Reynolds, if she was murdered, find the monster that did it. My wife and I were fixing dinner together at our home last night getting ready to entertain some fellow winery owners. It's a hobby of ours. We had our home outfitted with a commercial kitchen, since we both love to cook. Anyway, both of us were so shaken by the news, we couldn't concentrate on what we were doing, and we had our maid tell the guests that the dinner had been cancelled and the reason for it. Neither one of us would have enjoyed it, and it would have been very apparent to our guests."

Well, that means the maid could probably vouch that Signora Moretti was at home when Angela died. Guess she can be crossed off of the persons of interest list.

"*Signor*, do you mind if Sheriff Reynolds sits in on our meeting with Matteo?" Jim asked. "He's not met him, and I'm sure it would save both of them time. I have the feeling that you're going to want to bring Matteo up to speed immediately."

"Yes. I have no objection. I said hello to him when I walked in. He's sitting out on the porch with a woman I didn't recognize."

"That would probably be my wife," Mike said. "This may sound strange, *Signor*, but my wife seems to have a talent for solving murders. I know, I can see from the look on your face that it's kind of unusual. Believe me, it was nothing I wanted in a wife, but the bottom line is she's very good at it, and she'll be helping me. If she's sitting on the porch with Matteo, I would bet she's found out everything she can from him. For some reason, people open up to her far more than they do people in law enforcement."

"I'll get Matteo," Jim said.

CHAPTER TWENTY-ONE

Jim stepped out onto the porch and said, "Matteo, *Signor* Moretti is ready to meet with you. There is a man who will be sitting in on the meeting by the name of Sheriff Reynolds. He's representing Sheriff Dawson."

"That's fine. I've just spent some time sitting here on the porch with his wife. Jim, this is Kelly Reynolds, the sheriff's wife."

"Nice to meet you, Mrs. Reynolds," Jim said, extending his hand towards Kelly. "This shouldn't take too long. Your husband wanted to meet Matteo, and this will save time for everyone."

"That's fine. I'll just sit here and look out at the vineyard. It's quite beautiful."

"I couldn't agree more. Every time I look out at it, which is pretty often, it's like a mini-meditation time for me. It clears my head of whatever has been bothering me. Enjoy." With that, the two men walked into the building.

After introductions were made, *Signor* Moretti began to speak. "Matteo, I know we talked briefly last night, and I'm sorry to have to call this meeting so soon after the death of your wife. Believe me, I wish we both had more time to grieve, but as you well know when one is making wine, time is of the essence. So, let me get directly to the point. I want to hire you as the winemaker for the Moretti Winery effective immediately. I have several reasons for doing so. First of all, I know you. Your knowledge of wine is superb, as is your palate."

Matteo interrupted him. "I'm good, *Signor*, but let's not pretend. We both know Angela was better."

"Only slightly, Matteo, only slightly. There is no doubt in my mind that you can do every bit as fine a job with our grapes as she did. I am certain we will continue to produce the best wines in the valley. Naturally, I have told no one that I want to hire you, but the rumor mill has started."

"What do you mean, sir? About Angela?" Matteo asked, clasping his hands together as a worried look appeared on his face.

"No, Matteo. About who my new winemaker will be. Naturally you are the one who comes to most people's minds, but there are others who have called me. I must say the strangest call I've received was from the intern who has been working here."

"Caitlin called you? What did she want?" Jim asked with a sound of surprise in his voice.

"What do you think? She wanted to be the winemaker for the Moretti Winery," Gio replied as he suppressed a laugh. "She said she had the top grades in her studies at the university, and she had been interning here for over a month. She felt she could easily fill the job. She said she would drop out of school and finish her master's degree at a later date."

"You're kidding, right *Signor*?" Matteo said as his mouth fell open. "Angela said she was ambitious, and she thought it might be a problem for her, but that is amazing. It takes years to learn the language of the grapes. It's not something you can learn just from books."

"I agree, Matteo," Gio said with a wise nod. "I told her she had a long way to go before she'd be ready to be the winemaker at any winery, much less an award-winning one. Believe it or not, she told me I'd regret my decision and hung up on me. I remember staring at the phone in disbelief. I think we will have to find another intern, because even if she does return, I don't want her on my property."

"I'll call the dean of the department, *Signor,* and tell him what happened," Jim said. "He's a friend of mine, and maybe he can convince her that like wine, she needs to age a little."

"Thanks. Matteo, I would pay you what I paid Angela and naturally you may continue to live in the house I have provided here on the property. I know how awkward the timing is, but if you agree to take the job, you'll need to get started immediately."

"*Signor,* Sheriff Dawson took a lot of our files with him to see if there was anything of interest in them," Jim said as he turned to Mike and asked, "Think you could get those returned to us?"

"I'll go over to his office after I leave here," Mike said. "If he or his deputies haven't had a chance to go over them, I can. When I'm finished, I'll return them or have one of his deputies bring them back. Would that be all right with you?"

"Thank you, that would be great," *Signor* Moretti said. "Well, Matteo, are you ready to accept my offer and become the winemaker for the Moretti Winery?"

Matteo took a deep breath. "Yes, as I told the sheriff's wife earlier, being the winemaker at the Moretti Winery would be a dream come true, but now it's turned into a nightmare because of Angela's death. As much as I love making wine, it will be my job to put the nightmare portion of my dream behind me and concentrate on making the best wines in the valley. That will be Angela's legacy."

"Good. I feel very comfortable with you in that position. Let's go to Angela's office, or rather your office, and begin." *Signor* Moretti stood up and turned to Mike. "If I can help you in any way, please call me. If we assume that Angela was murdered, I want nothing more in the world than to have the demon who committed this horrible crime to be caught and punished."

"Rest assured sir, I will do everything in my power to see to it that the guilty party is brought to justice." They shook hands and Mike walked out to the porch where Kelly was waiting for him.

CHAPTER TWENTY-TWO

After Mike's meeting with *Signor* Moretti and Matteo, Kelly and Mike got in their rental car and left the winery. Kelly noticed that even though there had apparently been a murder at the vineyard the previous evening, the workers were walking up and down the rows of grapes, as if nothing had taken place. She knew that timing was everything in the wine business, but nevertheless it seemed strange.

Kelly turned to Mike, who was driving, and said. "What's on your agenda for the rest of the afternoon, honey? If you don't mind, I'd like to go back to the bed and breakfast and call Julia. I want to find out how Ella's doing. After that, I thought I might walk to the square and talk to the florist and the chocolatier, or maybe I'll go to the square first."

He looked over at her. "I won't even ask why for now. You can tell me about it over dinner, and I'll tell you about my conversations with Jim and *Signor* Moretti. By the way, Matteo accepted the job as winemaker and is starting right away. Sheriff Dawson's deputies removed a number of files from Angela's office, and they need to be returned to the winery. I don't know if you heard, but evidently there was a very bad accident on the highway leading into Sonoma. Several people died, and there are others in critical condition. My guess is that whole department has their hands full at the moment and going through those files will be on the back burner."

"What are you going to do with them?" Kelly asked.

"I know what Sheriff Dawson will be looking for, and I can spend a couple of hours looking at them. After I'm finished, I'll take them back to the winery and then meet you at our B & B. By the way, when you talk to Julia, see if she had some place in mind for dinner tonight, and tell her to give Ella my love."

"Will do," Kelly said, smiling. Mike's concern for little Ella was touching. "Why don't you take me to the square, and I won't bother going back to the room. I'll meet you back there when we've both finished."

"Good idea, and that will save me some time. I don't anticipate any problems with the files, but you never know."

Just after Mike turned onto the street across from the square, Kelly waved her arm, pointed, and said, "There's the flower shop, Mike. You can let me off here. Good luck. See you later," she said as she got out of the car and walked towards Paula's Posies.

The shop had tubs of beautiful colored flowers in front of it offset by a bright green door. She opened it and a small bell rang, indicating there was a customer. A moment later a woman who appeared to be in her mid-40's walked out of the back room, wearing gloves and an apron. Her greying hair was pulled back in a ponytail, and she smiled in greeting. "May I help you?"

"Yes, I'd like to talk to Paula for a moment. Would that be you?"

"Guilty as charged. What can I do for you?" Paula peeled off the gloves she was wearing and set them on the counter beside a pair of pruning shears.

"I'm trying to help Matteo Lucci," Kelly explained. "I'm sure you know that his wife, Angela, was found dead in a wine vat at the Moretti Winery last night. Sheriff Dawson suspects foul play may have been involved, and he's investigating her death as a possible homicide. My husband and I are visiting Sonoma. He's a sheriff in

Oregon, and I know from his cases that often the victim's spouse is the first one looked at as a suspect. Matteo reminds me of my son, and I'd like to help him clear his name. I understand he bought a bouquet from you yesterday evening."

"That's true. Please, have a seat. Actually, it was quite an undertaking. He was very specific in what he wanted, and I had to take several floral arrangements apart that I had made for delivery today. Fortunately, the flower grower I buy most of my flowers from was able to deliver more of the ones I needed."

"Matteo mentioned that he had an arrangement made that was very similar to the one his wife had carried down the aisle at their wedding. From what he told me, it sounded beautiful."

"It was. He has a very exacting eye, and he knew exactly what he wanted. He had trouble remembering a couple of the flowers, so that's one reason it took so long. I had to try several different kinds, before it was just the way he wanted it."

"I hate to ask this, but I know one of the sheriff's deputies would. Do you remember how long he was here and the approximate time?"

"Yes," Paula answered, "he was here from about 6:30 to 7:30. I remember because I close the shop at 6:30, and I had just turned the sign to closed when he knocked on the door. He's always been a good customer, as a matter of fact, he's bought a lot of bouquets from me in the past." She laughed and said, "He told me once that he and Angela were both hot-blooded Italians and arguing was a part of their life, but he said it was worth it when they made up. That's why he bought bouquets from me."

"Do you know if he went home or went anywhere else after he left your shop?" Kelly asked.

"He mentioned he was going to Nic's to get some chocolate truffles for Angela, but I can't tell you that with any certainty. When he left, I locked the door and went out the back way to where my van was parked, so I didn't see exactly where he went."

"Thank you for taking the time to talk to me. Could you point me in the direction of Nic's shop?"

"Yes, he's located across the square and down that side street," she said gesturing towards the street. "If you like chocolate, you'll not find a better shop."

"Again, thanks for your time and the information," Kelly said as she walked towards the door.

"I'm glad you're doing this," Paula said. "Even if Matteo is a bit hot-blooded, he's one of the finest people I've ever met, and while he and Angela may have argued from time to time, he worshipped her."

Kelly walked across the square and made her way down the street to a shop with the simple sign, "Gourmet Chocolate." She looked in the window as she walked to the door and saw several people standing in front of a long counter filled with what appeared to be different kinds of chocolates. She opened the door and walked in, inhaling what she considered to be a smell coming directly from heaven. When Kelly looked at the long, glass-enclosed counter, she couldn't believe the number of different kinds of chocolates the shop carried.

She looked at the vast array of sweets being offered and at their names: cacao, chocolate liquor, milk chocolate, white chocolate, cocoa, couverture, gianduja, single bean chocolate, and others, many of which were unfamiliar to her. As someone who had provided for her family by owning and operating a coffee shop after her husband had died, she thought she knew a lot about food, but this shop took it to a new level.

Kelly knew that chocolate making was considered to be an art form, but this shop seemed to take it beyond that. She couldn't help salivating at the sights and the smells in the shop, and thought it was a lovely touch that each purchase was wrapped in a gold foil box with a gold ribbon around it. A young woman seemed to be in charge of the wrapping, and an older man she heard several customers call Nic hurried to fill each customer's order.

Finally, it was Kelly's turn to be waited on. The man named Nic said, "Welcome. I don't think I've seen you in my shop before. How may I help you?" Since the other customers had left the shop, she told him what she'd told Paula a little earlier, specifically that she was trying to help Matteo clear his name.

"Whatever I can do to help Matteo, I will," Nic said solemnly. "*Dio lo benedica* – God bless him. You know, we come from the same town in Italy, and our families are friends, although he and I met for the first time here in Sonoma. He was here last night and bought truffles for Angela."

"That's what he told me. Do you remember what time it was?" Kelly asked.

"Yes. I stay open until 8:00, because so many people like to come here for a sweet after they've finished dinner rather than have dessert at a restaurant. When Matteo left I looked at my watch, and it was 8:00 on the dot. Several other people were still in the shop. They are all good customers and had waited while I helped Matteo, so I stayed later than usual. When they left the shop, I closed up and went home. If you would like their names, I could give them to you."

"No, I don't want to speak for Sheriff Dawson, but I don't think that will be necessary. Thank you anyway." Kelly turned to leave, but Nic called after her.

"I must tell you, we're all sick about what happened to Angela. She was loved by everyone that knew her, and we will all do whatever we can to help Matteo. He's fine young man."

"Nic, you've been most helpful." An afterthought occurred to her. "I almost forgot, but I do have one other question which has nothing to do with Matteo."

"If I can answer it, I would be happy to."

"My family and I had a wine tasting at the Moretti Winery yesterday afternoon, and there was a chocolate on our tasting platter that had been made with a wine from the winery. It was the best thing I've ever had. Does your shop make them for the winery?"

"Yes. Their wine is so extraordinary, it matched perfectly with one of my best chocolates. When Josie became the tour guide for the winery, she asked if I could come up with something special. I'm sure you noticed that on top of each chocolate there was an M and a W intertwined, the initials of the winery."

"I'm afraid I didn't notice. When I popped it into my mouth I was too busy thinking I'd never had anything that tasted that good. I would like to buy several boxes of them for friends of mine in Cedar Bay, Oregon. That's where I'm from, and I know they'd like them."

"Aah, that is a problem," Nic said with a sad shake of his head.

"Why?"

"You see, I made a promise to Josie that I would never sell them in the shop. The only way you can get those is at the Moretti Winery during a wine tasting, but I might have a treat for you, since you're helping my friend, Matteo." He raised a finger and smiled. "Wait."

He walked through a door into a back room. A moment later he came back with a Moretti chocolate on a napkin. "I promised Josie I would never sell them, but I never promised her I would not give one away occasionally. I would appreciate it if you kept it our secret." He bowed his head and handed the napkin to Kelly, who carefully tucked it into her purse.

"I do promise," she said, "but I would also be very remiss if I didn't take some of your chocolates back to Cedar Bay as gifts. I'd like to buy three boxes of mixed chocolates. I have no preferences, and you know far, far more about this subject than I do, so I'll rely on you to pick them out."

His assistant carefully filled the boxes, tying luxurious gold bows around them before presenting them to Kelly. "Nic, thank you for the information and for the chocolate, and believe me, I will recommend your shop to anyone who is planning to come to Sonoma."

"My pleasure, *Signora*, and please, do what you can to help Matteo. Do you think he'll be considered a suspect?"

"I can't speak for the sheriff, but I would be very surprised if he is." Everyone Kelly had met seemed to hold Matteo in high regard, and from what Kelly could tell, he was just a hot-headed Italian who was a lover, not a fighter. "You and Paula have given him an alibi, and I feel certain other people will be looked at, even though the sheriff is waiting for the coroner's report to determine if Angela's health was a cause of death or if there was a foreign substance in her body."

"She was in perfect health, and as far as alcohol and drugs, that is not even a possibility. No, I believe she was murdered. But who would want to kill her?" he asked, turning the palms of his hands up in a gesture of resignation.

"I don't know Nic, but I feel certain that the person will be found and hopefully, sooner rather than later."

CHAPTER TWENTY-THREE

As soon as Kelly left Nic's, she took the chocolate piece he'd given her out of the napkin it was wrapped in and put it in her mouth. It made her feel like she was floating on a chocolate cloud all the way back to the B & B where they were staying. She didn't see Mike's car in the parking lot, so she figured he was still either looking at files or at the winery.

When she got to their room, she carefully placed the gold-wrapped boxes containing the chocolates she'd purchased in the small refrigerator in their room. Even though it was a cool day, after paying what the chocolates had cost her, not an inexpensive amount, she didn't want to take the chance that they might melt. She was already concerned about having to put them in her luggage on the flight back to Portland.

She called Julia, and a moment later heard her voice say, "Hi, Mom. Figured you'd call sometime today. Before you even ask, I'll fill you in on Ella. She has strep throat. The doctor put her on antibiotics, and we've been giving her baby aspirin. Her fever is down, but her throat is raw. Poor little thing. We definitely made the right decision in coming home. What's going on with you two, and sorry to bail on you."

Kelly spent the next few minutes telling Julia about Mike and his golf game, Angela's death, their conversation with Sheriff Dawson, her talk with Matteo, and her visits to Paula's Posies and Nic's.

"Good grief, Mom. I can't leave you alone for a minute without something major happening to you. That's too bad about Angela. I liked her when I met her. I'm sure Josie is devastated."

"That's an understatement," Kelly sighed. "Not only is Josie a wreck right now, a lot of other people are too. She seemed to really be liked here in Sonoma."

"Mom, I know you've been involved in a number of Mike's cases. What's your feeling about this one?"

"As soon as I met Matteo, I felt he was innocent. Maybe because of Cash I'm a sucker for young men that remind me of your brother, but it was just too obvious. As far as who did it? I don't know. Mike's at the sheriff's station reading the Moretti Winery files, so he might know something when he gets back. I do know the sheriff was hoping to have a preliminary coroner's report and fingerprint analysis completed by later today or tonight. Maybe those will show something, but it seems to me anyone who went to that much trouble to come up with a plan to kill Angela, isn't going to leave a trail of fingerprints."

"I wouldn't think so, either. Mom, I'm going to have to go in a minute. I think Ella just woke up from her nap, and I need to give her some medicine. I haven't told the girls about Disneyland yet. Do you think Mike was serious about taking them?"

"Absolutely." Kelly knew the big kid in Mike was just glad that Julia had brought up the subject of Disneyland, since he'd been talking about going there ever since she'd met him. "We'll work out the details later. Oh, Julia, I did get that wine information for you from Josie. I'll mail it to you."

"That was nice of her. I'm sure she had a lot more important things to think about. Mom, you could do me one favor tomorrow."

There was nothing Kelly wouldn't do for her daughter. "Consider it done, sweetheart. What is it?"

"There's a wine tasting room on the square that I'd like you to visit. Try a couple of wines, or have Mike try them, and see what you think. If you like them and think I would, please buy a couple of bottles and have them sent to me. Can you do that?"

"Sure, honey. I don't have anything on my agenda for tomorrow, and we're not leaving until the next day. What's the name of the winery?"

"It's called the Romano Winery. I understand they're a close second to the Moretti Winery. I've never tried their wines, but if they're anything like what we had at the Moretti Winery, I'll probably like them."

Kelly was quiet, thinking what a small world it was. What were the chances that the one winery's wine her daughter wanted her to try was the very one where Matteo had been the winemaker? She decided not to say anything for now.

"Sure, Julia. Are you thinking of something special?"

"Not really. Why don't you try a red and a white and if you like them, I'll take them as an early birthday gift."

"Will do. One last thing, and then you need to go check on Ella. Any thoughts on where we should have dinner tonight? You're the one who did all the research before we came, so I thought you might have the name of a place."

"How did you know?" Kelly heard Julia's tinkling laughter at the other end of the line. "As a matter of fact, I do. It's name is The Pastel Rose, and it's on the square. The chef named it that because guess what? He loves pastel roses. They're his favorite flowers, and according to what I read, there are always fresh roses on every table and some beautiful floral paintings on the walls. I saw an online photo of the restaurant and it looked gorgeous."

"Sounds beautiful. Even if we can't get a reservation there, I'd like to walk by and see it. I love how you always come up with the best places. You're so thoughtful."

"Mom, they're known for their farm fresh food. Their claim to fame is they only serve organic food and from what I read, their chef is known to be one of the best. I believe he had a very successful cooking show on television for several years. He got tired of the whole chef stardom world and opened the restaurant. You're the food expert, let me know what you think."

"You've got me chomping at the bit already. We'll go there for dinner tonight, if we can. I better call and make a reservation if he's that good. Grandpa said to be sure and tell the girls hi for him. I'll call you tomorrow and see how Ella's doing. Loves," Kelly said as she ended the call. She immediately called The Pastel Rose and made a reservation for 7:00 that night.

CHAPTER TWENTY-FOUR

There was a knock on the door and then the sound of someone entering the room. Kelly was in the bathroom putting on some makeup. Fixing a smudge of mascara on her cheek, she paused and cocked her ear. "Mike, is that you?"

"Yes, were you expecting someone else?" he asked.

She peered through the open bathroom door. "Maybe, but I'm glad you got here first. You look tired." She walked out of the bathroom and let him hold her before wriggling away when he tried to kiss her.

"Sorry, but you'll ruin my lipstick. I talked to Julia and Ella has strep throat, so I'm glad they decided to go home. She gave me the name of a restaurant that's supposed to be pretty good, so I made a reservation there for dinner at 7:00. Since it's on the square, we can walk to it. That gives us about a half an hour."

"Good." Mike gave Kelly an admiring glance. "In that case, you better get dressed. I could use a couple of minutes to unwind." He sank into one of the armchairs and started to take off his shoes. "What a day this turned out to be. A complete reversal of what I thought it was going to be when I got up this morning."

"I agree," Kelly said as she kissed the top of his head before disappearing back into the bathroom. "Take a few minutes to decompress, and I won't bother you. We can talk over dinner."

"Kelly, Kelly, Kelly, don't you know you never bother me. I love your chatter and your view of the world. Believe me, it's pretty refreshing from the world I usually find myself in."

"Thanks for the compliment, sweetheart. I'll remind you of that the next time you roll your eyes over something I've said. I'll be out of here in a couple of minutes, and the bathroom will be all yours."

A few minutes later she walked out and saw Mike slouched in the chair, his eyes closed. She softly touched his cheek and said, "Wake up, sleeping beauty. The bathroom is all yours, Sheriff."

Mike's mouth twitched and his eyelids flickered. "Thanks. I'm kind of lagging, and a little fresh water on my face will do wonders for my attitude, to say nothing of the glass of wine I plan on having with dinner."

"Kind of getting into this Sonoma thing, aren't you?" Kelly asked with a grin on her face.

"Well, I'm a great believer of when in Rome…" He tried to pull Kelly onto his lap, but she dodged his grasp once more.

"Nice excuse, Sheriff, but from what Julia told me, we should be in for a gastronomic treat tonight."

Mike grunted. "From that I take it I should bring all the credit cards I have, and you might want to do the same. Living a glossy magazine lifestyle on a sheriff's paycheck is a tall order, Mrs. Reynolds. Remember when Liz and Doc went to Spain a few months ago on a bucket list trip?"

"Yes, what about it?" Kelly asked.

"Because their bill at the Michelin five star rated restaurant in the seaside town of San Sebastian was over $700.00 and that didn't include their wine. That was on a separate bill. Doc said he figured he'd have to start doubling up on his patient load to pay for that dinner."

"Somehow, I doubt it," Kelly said, stepping into a black halter dress and pulling it down over her hips. She slipped on the jacket and looked in the mirror, smiling at her reflection. "I know doctors and psychologists earn a lot more in big cities, but I think Liz and Doc could afford it, although it's a matter of priorities. I love food, but I think if I saw those prices on a menu, I'd leave."

"From what Doc told me, there weren't any prices on the menu."

"That would make me worry before I'd even ordered."

*****

Later, after a short walk to the restaurant, they held hands and as they were looking in the window of The Pastel Rose, Kelly inhaled sharply. Mike glanced over at her and said, "Kelly, what's wrong?"

"Absolutely nothing, Mike. This is simply one of the most beautiful restaurants I've ever seen. Take another look inside," she said as she continued to peer through the window. "There are candles everywhere, and they've mixed up the table linens so they're all in different pastel colors. I guess that's to match the name of the restaurant. I think we're in for a wonderful experience."

He opened the door for her and guided her inside with his hand in the small of her back. "At the risk of sounding like a wet blanket, I sincerely hope it's not the same experience that Doc and Liz had in Spain."

Kelly was so busy taking in the feast of colors and scents when they walked into the restaurant, she didn't respond. Mike gave their name to the hostess and they were quickly seated at a window table that looked out at the square. A waiter appeared, deftly unfolded Kelly's napkin as if he were a magician, and handed it to her. It was a soft pink color. The tablecloth was a cream-colored linen and in the center of the table was a short bouquet of lavender roses bursting out of a sparkling crystal vase. Kelly looked around and saw that the other tables repeated the color scheme, depending on what color the center bouquets were.

Kelly had heard that in addition to Sonoma being known as a wine mecca, there was also a very active art colony living and working in the area. The paintings on the walls spoke to that industry. Soft floral paintings of pastel roses hung on the white walls, accenting the table bouquets. The prices shown on some of the painting indicated they were for sale. Red dots on some of the others indicated that they had already been sold.

"Mike, I wasn't kidding earlier. This really is one of the most beautiful restaurants I've ever been in." Kelly's gaze settled on one of the paintings, and Mike gave her a sharp warning look.

"Good, I'm glad you like it, because I just looked at the wine prices, and not only do I not have a clue what any of the wines are, we could probably retire on the prices being charged on a couple of the bottles. It's a good thing we hardly drink. Where's Julia when we need her?"

A man walked over to the table and introduced himself. "Welcome to The Pastel Rose. My name is Armand. May I help you select a wine?"

"I don't know where to start," Mike said. "I'm afraid I'm nowhere near knowledgeable enough to order something on my own, so yes, I could use a little help."

"Very well, sir. Do you have an idea of what you'll be ordering from the dinner menu?"

"No, I haven't had a chance to look at it yet."

"Sir, if I may make a suggestion, since you don't seem to have a definite preference, the chef has a tasting menu tonight which consists of an appetizer, soup, salad, an entrée, and dessert. From what I'm hearing from the other diners, it's very, very good. I could pair wines for the different courses."

"I think that would solve my problem, but neither my wife nor I are very big drinkers. Could we share a glass instead of each of us having one?

"Of course, sir, but I will divide the wine into two glasses. It would really be tacky for you both to be seen passing a glass of wine back and forth, and I think Chef Antoine would have an apoplectic fit if he walked into the dining room and saw that. Shall I place a tasting order for both of you?"

"Kelly, is that alright with you?" Mike asked.

"It sounds wonderful, Armand. We'll trust your judgement."

"Thank you, *Madame*, and I promise that it will be an experience you will long remember." He smiled and walked away from the table.

"What do you think, Mike?" she asked. "He handled that impeccably, in my opinion."

"I think that's probably what somebody told Doc before he went down the rabbit hole in Spain. Did you bring your credit cards?"

"Yes, but you said you had yours."

"So I did, but you didn't see the wine selections on the menu that the hostess gave me. There were only a couple of prices on it and I have a feeling those were the cheap ones. I know it's going to be shades of Doc and Liz."

"Well, if it is, it is." Kelly reached out for his hand and gave it a reassuring squeeze across the creamy linen tablecloth. "Let's forget about the money part and just enjoy the experience. We won't be passing this away again."

"Trust me," Mike warned her. "We won't be able to afford to pass this way again."

"No more grumbling," Kelly said, retracting her hand as a waiter brought over plates and set them in front of each of them. He was followed by the sommelier who placed two small glasses of wine on the table at the top of their knives.

"The chef is starting out your tasting menu with a Spanish favorite. Enjoy," the waiter said as he left their table.

"Mike, this looks too beautiful too eat," Kelly said as she surveyed the sliced red tomatoes on baguettes which had been sprinkled with chopped basil.

Mike hadn't paused to admire the view. "It's even better than it looks. What do you think the chef has done?" He asked with his mouth half full.

"Good thing your granddaughters aren't here," she said, picking up her fork. "I believe you were the one who told them it's bad manners to talk with food in your mouth."

"So I did, but this is just too good not to know exactly what I'm eating."

Kelly took a bite and waited as her taste buds sprang into action and did their thing of deciphering the ingredients. "Mike, I'm pretty sure I can make this at home and at the coffee shop. Tastes like a little olive oil, balsamic vinegar, and a special salt has been sprinkled on top of the tomatoes. I'm a sucker for a good olive oil, balsamic vinegar, and gourmet salt. I think anything would taste good with those on it."

For the next hour conversation was at a minimum as they devoured the tasting menu which, in addition to the appetizer, consisted of an apple-butternut squash soup, quinoa salad, rosemary roasted chicken with fingerling potatoes, and for dessert, a cheesecake with caramelized peaches. Mike had just sat back in his chair and was enjoying an after-dinner cup of decaf coffee when his phone buzzed.

"Kelly, it's Sheriff Dawson. I noticed there was a sign when we came in that indicated cell phones should be put on vibrate. I'm going to step outside to take his call. If he's calling this time of night, it's probably important."

He walked outside and through the window Kelly could see him pacing back and forth on the sidewalk. A few minutes later he returned with a worried look on his face. He sat down a took a sip from his cup of coffee.

"Mike, I can see from the worried look on your face that whatever the sheriff told you, it probably wasn't good news," Kelly said.

"I don't think it's ever good news when the verdict is murder. The coroner's preliminary report came back, and there were no signs of health problems and only a small trace of alcohol was found in Angela's body, but no drugs."

"Well, given the fact that her body was found in a wine vat, that's not surprising, since from what we've been told, she took a small sip from each of the vats."

"Yes, but there's more. There were two sets of shoe prints on the stairs leading up to the top of the vat. One was matched with a pair of Angela's shoes. The other was a very small set of prints and from what Dawson told me, they were made from a type of shoe that many people in the wine industry wear. Not the vineyard workers, because they need heavy duty boots, but people like Josie or others, the ones who were in and out of the vineyards and buildings.

Kelly looked at him and said, "Matteo told me about them earlier today. He said most of the people wore them because they could slip them off when they entered a building. That way they didn't track mud and dirt into the building."

"Matteo was wearing a pair of sandals when we met earlier, but I think he had big feet. Dawson said the shoeprint appeared to be about a size four, narrow, which is quite small."

"Does that mean you think it belonged to a woman?"

"It would certainly seem to indicate that, but it could have been a small man. I don't know, but it's a very important clue."

"A clue, yes, but not enough to charge someone with murder. Right?"

"That's right, but that circumstantial evidence, along with some other evidence, might be enough to do it. Why?"

Kelly sipped her coffee, which had become cold while she was waiting for Mike to return. "Matteo told me there's a shoe store on the square where most of the people who work in the wine industry and wanted sandals like his like to shop. It's too late tonight, but I think I'll go there when they open in the morning and see what I can find out."

"Not a bad idea. What would you think if I tried to play golf in the morning? The two guys I played with today said they had a really early tee time, 7:00 a.m., and that if I could make it, to just meet them at the first tee."

"I think that would be wonderful." Kelly said as she tried to get the waiter's attention for the check. "This was supposed to be a vacation, and as hard as you work, I'd like to see you relax."

"Same goes for you, Kelly. How about if I take the car to the course in the morning and you sleep in? You could walk to the square when the shoe store opens, and then we could go to lunch when I get back."

"Sounds great. Julia had one request for us. She asked if we would go to the Romano Winery tasting room on the square and try a red and a white wine. She said if they're any good, she'd like us to buy a couple of bottles of each of them and have them shipped to her in Calico Gold."

Kelly paused while the waiter set the check on the table. She was delighted to see it was accompanied by two of Nic's gourmet chocolates on a little dish. She hoped that would soften the blow when Mike paid the bill. "I looked it up on my iPad while I was waiting for you earlier and they have food as well at the Romano Winery Tasting Room. Let's go there for lunch and we can get that out of the way."

"Perfect. Let me settle up here, and we can go get a good night's sleep. Feels like it's been a very long day." He flipped open the check and barely flinched.

Kelly sat in her chair waiting for some indication from Mike about how much the meal and wine had cost. He signed the credit card slip and said, "Ready, Mrs. Reynolds?"

"Yes, but I'm curious what this gastronomic feast cost," she said as she walked towards the door with him.

"Isn't there some saying about how curiosity killed the cat? Let's just say it's a good thing you handle the books for the coffee shop, and I handle the books for our household. I think you'll enjoy the evening far more if you don't know the cost. I think there's another saying that's appropriate. If you have to ask, you can't afford it. Let's just say we could afford it, and let it go at that."

"That's probably good advice. I'd hate to get indigestion."

CHAPTER TWENTY-FIVE

"Good luck with your golf game, Mike," Kelly mumbled from under the covers. "They start serving breakfast downstairs at 6:00, so you can either grab a quick bite there or take something with you to eat on the course."

"Thanks, Kelly. I'm a big boy, and I promise I won't let myself starve," he said grinning as he leaned down and kissed her. "Go back to sleep. The town's quiet, and the shoe store won't open for a few more hours. You can use a little down time. Enjoy it, and I'll meet you back here around noon. Loves." He closed the door softly behind him as he headed for their car in the parking lot.

Kelly took his advice, rolled over, and promptly went back to sleep. She woke up two hours later and looked at the alarm clock on the nightstand on Mike's side of the bed.

Wow. I really did go back to sleep. Guess all that good food needed a little more time to settle in. Time for a shower and some breakfast, although as much as I had to eat last night, think it will be very, very light.

After she'd showered and dressed, she walked down the stairs to the dining room. The buffet was still set up, but judging by the empty room, everyone else who was staying at the B and B had already eaten. She walked over to a window table and sat down, admiring the display of colorful flowers in the garden outside her window.

A young woman walked over with a coffee pot and said, "May I serve you some coffee?"

"Yes, thank you. Those flowers are beautiful, but I'm surprised at how healthy and colorful they are at this time of year." Kelly watched as the waitress poured and took her first sip of coffee of the day, which was always the best.

"The owners love butterflies, and one of the flowers in particular, is very butterfly-friendly."

"I'm not that familiar with them. If we have them in Oregon, I've never planted them, but I'd love to have some butterflies in my yard. Can you tell me what they are?"

"Yes. You're not the first guest to be captivated by them, so I've had to learn. The purple ones are agastache. They're the ones the butterflies like the best. We also have peonies, delphinium, and sedum. These flowers like cool rainy weather as well, so they'll be here most of the winter. They are beautiful, aren't they?"

"Exquisite. You must enjoy working in such a beautiful environment."

"I love my job. I'm a student at Sonoma State University. Have you had a chance to see it?"

"No, this is my first time here. Why?"

"It's been ranked as having the most beautiful campus of any college in the United States. I like beautiful things in nature, which is probably why I like working here. I'm hoping to go to the University of California at Davis next year and study winemaking."

"From what I've seen since I've been here, that industry seems to support this valley."

"That it does, and I'd like the chance to work and be outside in the vineyards. It seems like a perfect thing for me to do career-wise.

Anyway, please help yourself to our buffet. The chef is very good, and I think you'll enjoy it."

"Regretfully, I'll probably only have a bagel or a piece of toast. I'm still full from the meal I had last night."

"May I ask where you ate?"

"Yes, we ate at The Pastel Rose, and we had the tasting menu. I should have just had a salad."

The young woman laughed. "You did well. Chef Armand is considered to be the best in the valley, and the tasting menu allows him to really show what he can do. I can't afford to eat there, but someday I plan to."

"My husband told me I'd be better off not knowing how much we spent on dinner, so that, in conjunction with what you're saying, leads me to agree with him." Kelly smiled up at the waitress. "Thanks for talking to me. I've learned a lot from you. Good luck in your studies."

"Enjoy the rest of your stay," she said as she walked away.

Kelly walked over to the buffet table and couldn't resist taking the lids off the various serving dishes to see what was in them. The only thing that kept her from indulging in the superb looking food was the thought that she really did need to talk to someone at the shoe store, and if she was sick to her stomach from overeating, it probably would not be a good thing for either her or whomever she talked to. Reluctantly, she took a piece of dry sourdough bread and lightly toasted it. Her hand hovered over the freshly made peach jam, but as difficult as it was for a foodie, she resisted the temptation.

When she was finished eating, she walked out to the reception area and asked the young man at the desk if he knew where the Sonoma Shoe Salon was located.

"It's on the town square, about a half a block down from a

restaurant called The Pastel Rose. It's got a big sign hanging out from the wall with a shoe on it. You can't miss it."

"Thanks," Kelly said. Since she already had her purse with her, she started walking towards the square. A few minutes later she saw the sign along with a sign on the door that said "open." She walked into the shoe store and looked at various different shoes while she waited for the white-haired clerk to finish up with a customer.

She was kneeling down in front of a pair of sandals similar to the ones Matteo had worn the day before when a voice asked, "How may I help you today?" She stood up and turned to the woman who was dressed in black slacks with a black turtleneck under a brightly colored jacket that looked as if it had been made in Africa. Kelly recognized it from a catalogue she received which had similar clothes in it.

"I love your jacket," she said. "It's so colorful, it makes me happy."

"Thank you. That's exactly why I bought it. I'm glad you agree with me. Are you interested in buying some sandals?"

"I might be. I've seen several people in Sonoma wearing this type of sandal, and I was wondering if it was particularly comfortable or what."

"It's probably our bestselling sandal. I'm the owner of this shoe store, and my husband and I also own a small vineyard. We found that when we were pruning the grapes or doing other work outdoors, our shoes really got dirty, and we didn't want to wear them into the house. I'd have to unlace them and take them off, then in ten minutes or however long it was before I went outside again, I'd have to lace them back up. The long and short of it was that it took a lot of time.

"I decided to try a pair of sandals with socks and see how that would work. You'll notice these have a Velcro band on the back, so they can be slipped on an off easily. Other people began to notice what I was wearing, and one thing led to another. Now I sell more of these sandals than any other type of shoe we have here in the store. Almost everyone who works in the local wine industry, other than the people who work exclusively in the vineyards and need boots, wear them. As you can see, they come in several colors. What size do you wear?"

"I wear a pretty standard size, a seven. I'd like to try on a pair. Do you have a dark blue?"

"That I do. Have a seat, and I'll get a pair from the back. Actually, that size is the most popular," she said as she walked through the curtain to the back room.

When she returned, Kelly tried on the sandals. "These really are comfortable. No wonder they're so popular. I own a coffee shop in Cedar Bay, Oregon, and I'm on my feet a lot. I bet these would work well for me. I'll take them." Kelly wondered if she should get a pair for Roxie as well, but decided against it. Mike might have something to say about her generosity, and anyway, it wasn't often she bought something that no one else in Cedar Bay had. *Who knows*, she thought, *maybe I'll start a new craze.*

"I don't think you'll regret your purchase. As I said, I sell more of these than anything else. I can barely keep them in stock."

"I'd think that would be a problem, considering that your shop is not all that big. What do you do if someone wears a strange size?"

"I have to special order them from the manufacturer, but that's pretty rare. I can't waste my limited storage space with really big shoes or really small ones."

"I'm so used to this size, and my daughter wears the same size, so I've never considered that some people might be at either end of the shoe size spectrum. What's the smallest size you've ever sold, other than to a child?"

"A woman was in here several months ago, and she requested a red colored size four of this sandal. That is really tiny, but she was a very small woman, so it wasn't surprising to me that she wore a size four."

"Does she continue to buy from you?" Kelly asked innocently.

"No, I only sold her the one pair. As a matter of fact, when they were delivered to the store and I called her to let her know they were in, she told me someone else would pick them up for her, because she was tied up with a project. I didn't ask what it was, and that was the last time I talked to her. She paid in cash when she ordered the sandals. Very few shoe stores carry these, and the manufacturer doesn't even allow them to be sold on Amazon."

Kelly turned the sandals over and looked at the sole on the bottom. "These have quite a distinctive pattern of ridges on the bottom. Do they wear down with use?"

"A little. The company that makes these sandals does an interesting thing with their soles. All the sizes of one color have the same soleprint. They're kind of like a fingerprint. I was curious why the owner would do something like that. Seemed like an unnecessary process."

"What was the reason?"

"You have to realize the owner of the shoe company that makes these sandals is kind of a non-businesslike person. He felt the sandals should be distinctive, and even though they all resemble one another, the pattern on the sole makes them different, and he's right. If soleprints were taken from two different pairs of these sandals, unless they were the exact same color, the soleprints would be different."

"I've never heard of anything like that," Kelly said.

"Nor had I, but the fact that people are willing to pay what these sandals cost, tells me the owner knew what he was doing."

"So, theoretically if a soleprint was found, you could match that soleprint with one of these sandals and from that determine the color of the sandal that made it. Am I understanding you correctly?"

"Pretty much," the woman said. "If you showed me a soleprint made by these types of sandals, it would be easy for me to tell you what color the sandal was that made that soleprint."

"Well, I guess when you own a company you can do whatever you want, and it looks like he did," Kelly said. "I think I'm going to like these, and I've never seen sandals like these anywhere else. If I wanted to order another pair, would I just call you?"

"Yes. The phone number of my store is on the receipt. Is there anything else you'd like to see?" she asked as two customers walked in the front door.

"No, thanks. I'm so glad I bought these, and I'm really looking forward to wearing them. You'll probably be hearing from me."

"I'll look forward to it."

CHAPTER TWENTY-SIX

Kelly looked at her watch and decided to take a walk around the square. Although she'd visited several stores adjacent to the square, she'd never taken a full turn around it. The square consisted of a small grassy park in the center with each of the shops on the four sides of the square facing the park. A small wooden bandstand stood in the middle of the green. It presented a nice opportunity to walk and window shop.

She noticed there were a number of restaurants and tasting rooms and thought, as she had often before, that whenever winegrowing was the major focus of an area, good food was a natural accompaniment. It certainly was that way in the Willamette Valley in Oregon, not that far from her home in Cedar Bay. She and Mike had taken several weekend trips there, more for the food than the wine.

She'd almost completed her walk when her attention was caught by a sign for a kitchen shop. She remembered Julia had mentioned that there was one on the square. Given that cooking was such a large part of her life, she couldn't resist entering the shop. She spent a half hour meandering down each aisle, knowing she could spend a small fortune if she allowed herself to, but also knowing she couldn't carry much back with her on the plane and the amount necessary to ship the items lessened her desire to buy. Even so, she came away with a number of ideas and couldn't resist a cookbook entitled "Best of Sonoma Cookbook," particularly since the author was Chef Armand, the chef at The Pastel Rose.

After Kelly returned to their room at the B & B, she was just putting the cookbook in her carry-on bag so she could look at it while she was on the plane the following day, when the door opened and a grinning Mike entered.

Kelly looked at him and said, "I take it from that smile it was another good day on the golf course. Would I be right?"

"I don't know what's come over me, Kelly. We might have to move here. I did even better than yesterday. I can't believe it. It must be the course, because I sure can't think of anything I'm doing differently."

"The Cedar Bay public course is going to seem pretty hum-hum after two days on the Sonoma Golf Club course."

"You've got that right. I was wondering when I was driving here if it's the golf clubs. The ones I rented were really good. Maybe I need to get a new set. I've had the ones at home for a long, long time."

"Mike, I don't know a thing about golf clubs. Are they expensive?"

He was quiet for a few moments. "I'm trying to think how to phrase this. Could we say what we spent last night for dinner we did because you own a coffee shop and needed to get new ideas for your menu? Maybe we could write the cost of the dinner off as a business expense on our tax return. If we did that I could justify the cost of my new clubs."

"That expensive, huh?" she asked, zipping up her carry-on bag.

"Yeah."

"I think we better table this discussion for another time. Change your clothes and let's go eat. I had a very light breakfast this morning, and I'm ready for lunch."

*****

When they were outside, Mike walked towards the parking lot and beeped the car key fob in the air in the direction of the car. "Kelly, I'd like to stop by the sheriff's station after we finish lunch and the tasting for Julia, so I'm going to drive to the square rather than walk."

"Sure, that's fine. Hopefully, he's found out something by now. I'd think the initial investigation of that terrible traffic accident would be finished by now."

A few minutes later they walked into the Romano Winery Tasting Room on the far side of the square. Kelly noticed two security guards standing next to the front door and thought that was interesting. She figured the wines they served must be pretty pricey. Kelly looked around and thought whoever had designed the interior had done a wonderful job. Chairs and sofas in earthy colored plaids had been arranged in seating groups with low oak tables in front of them. The vibe was one of laid back elegance, and since it was lunch time, many people were eating as well as tasting wine.

At the rear of the very large room was a horseshoe shaped oak bar with stools upholstered in the same plaids as the chairs and sofas. Oak paneling covered the walls and canned lights hung from the ceiling, bathing the room in a soft glow. A hostess was seated at an antique desk in the middle of the room with a computer on her desk.

"Welcome. May I help you?" she asked.

Mike spoke up. "My wife and I would like to do a winetasting and have some lunch."

"Certainly, sir, but the only seats I have available at the moment are at the bar. As you can see, this is a busy time for us."

"No problem. You don't need to get up. I see two seats on the far side of the bar." He and Kelly walked over, pulled out bar stools, and sat down.

A tired looking young woman with a blond ponytail and dark circles under her eyes walked over to them and said, "Would you like to do a flight of wine, or individual glasses? And would you like to see our luncheon menu? It's not very extensive, but people seem to like it."

"I think we'll pass on the flight," Mike said. "I'd like a glass of your best red, and my wife would like your best white. And yes, we would like to see the menu. Thank you."

A moment later she came back, handed each of them a menu, and then returned with a glass of red wine and a glass of white wine. "Let me tell you a little about each of these wines."

"Thank you, we're not connoisseurs, so we'd appreciate it."

"The white wine is a sauvignon blanc blend. It has a crisp texture and layers of flavor including lemongrass, citrus, and melon. It's very refreshing, particularly on a warm summer day. The red wine is a blend of several grapes which give it an aroma of raspberry and spice with the smooth flavor of berries. It has soft supple tannins to finish it." From the way the descriptions rolled off of the woman's tongue in a monotone, Kelly thought she'd memorized the words, or maybe her delivery style came with the boredom of repeating the same thing over and over.

"Although any time is the right time to drink this wine, I personally prefer it when the weather is a little cooler. I'll be back in a moment to take your luncheon order."

Kelly looked at Mike and started to giggle. "Did you understand anything robot woman said? That was so far over my head. Maybe Julia would know what she was talking about, but I sure didn't."

"Sweetheart, I just took a sip of the red, and I didn't get a taste of anything other than it was good, and by the way, I haven't a clue what a tannin is. I think we should just tell Julia we're hopeless."

"I have a feeling she already thinks that's the case. Mike, I enjoyed the cheese platter we had at the winery so much, let's split the charcuterie platter. It's got three kinds of cheese, bread, prosciutto, mortadella, and an assortment of pickles and jams. How does that sound?"

"Perfect."

The young woman who was waiting on them walked over and said, "If you're uncertain about what to get, a lot of people come here specifically for the charcuterie platter. It's really good."

"Thanks, we'll share that. I assume it's enough for both of us," Kelly said.

"It certainly is. I'll be back in a few minutes with your plates and napkins."

Mike turned to face his wife. "Kelly, how was your morning? We talked about my golf game, but I believe you said you were going to go to the shoe store this morning."

"I did, and it was very interesting." She told him about her conversation with the owner and that she'd bought a pair of the sandals like the wine people seemed to prefer.

"What a strange thing. I wonder if Sheriff Dawson knows about the distinctive soleprints on those types of sandals. Let's be sure and tell him when we go there."

"Okay. Looks like lunch is here," she said as the young woman placed a large platter between their two plates. "This looks wonderful," Kelly said to her. "I'm looking forward to it."

"Well, let's put it this way. If you don't enjoy it, I think you'll be the first person who hasn't." She walked over to where two men and women were sitting with five wine glasses in front of them and carefully poured wine into the second glass in front of each of them. They could hear her explaining to the foursome the exact same details about one of the wines she'd just poured for them.

A few minutes later a beautiful young woman walked up to the bar and waited until their server had left the foursome. They spoke for a couple of minutes and then the young woman took off her red sandals and put them on the floor next to the bar, not far from where Kelly and Mike were sitting.

For several minutes, Kelly and Mike enjoyed their lunch with an occasional sip of wine. "Kelly, you have to try this cheese and this meat. They're amazing. I also recommend this jam. The combination is really good. This is something else I bet you could serve at the coffee shop. I know Josie said she was going to give you the information on the different cheeses we had at the winery. Did she?"

"She did, but I haven't had a chance to look at it. This is excellent, but if you'll excuse me for a moment, I need to go to the restroom. I'll be back in a minute."

"Okay, I'll pay while you're gone, and then we can head over to the sheriff's station. After that I might take a little nap. Between the big dinner last night and the golf game this morning, to say nothing of wine with lunch, it sounds like a good idea. Actually, I don't see our server, so I guess I'll have to wait until she returns from wherever she went. See you in a few minutes."

Kelly followed the sign that indicated the restrooms were down the hall and opened the door to the ladies' room. She heard someone talking from one of the two stalls and thought how strange it was that people would feel the need to talk to someone on their phone when they were in a restroom. She entered the other stall and locked the door.

"Lexie, I tell you something is really off with Alessandra. The last two nights she's been having nightmares and crying out in her sleep. I haven't gotten any shut eye, and I'm exhausted. It's kind of freaking me out. She keeps saying she killed someone, and it was all for nothing. It was something about how she'd called some guy named Matteo and told him that they could get together now that his wife was dead. She screamed that he'd told her he wanted nothing to do with her and hung up on her. It was pretty garbled, but that's pretty much the gist of what she said."

At the word, Matteo, Kelly's attention was immediately riveted on the conversation. It was quiet in the adjoining stall for a few moments and then the voice, which she recognized as being that of their server, saying, "She's here now. She just went into her uncle Carlos' office. Matter of fact, she left her sandals by the bar, because he won't allow anyone to walk on his Oriental rug with their shoes on. Anyway, I don't know what to do. I don't think I can spend another night with her. I get off work pretty soon, and I'm seriously thinking about packing up and getting the heck out of Dodge."

Again, it was quiet, then she heard the server say, "Thanks, Lexie. I really appreciate it. Honest, it will just be a for a few nights until I figure out what to do. I'm happy to sleep on the couch. See you after I finish my shift."

Kelly didn't make a sound. A minute later she heard the door to the restroom close. She waited several more minutes then crept out of the restroom. Down the hall, she saw a door with the words "Carlos Romano" on it. She heard a woman's loud, nearly hysterical voice, coming from the room. She walked a few feet down the hall to see if she could hear what was being said, wondering if the raised woman's voice was that of Alessandra.

"You're the one who suggested that Angela might fall into the vat," the voice screamed. "Remember when Matteo and I were here? Why are you acting so high and mighty with me about it now? No one will ever know it was me."

Kelly heard a man talking in low tones, as if he was trying to calm the woman down, but she couldn't make out his words. She didn't want to get any closer to the door, because she was afraid of being caught eavesdropping.

When she returned to the tasting room Mike was standing by his stool, waiting for her. "We have to leave now," he said in an urgent tone of voice, yanking her by the arm. "Start walking. I'll tell you all about it on the way to the B and B."

"Ouch! I thought we were going to the sheriff's station."

"No, there's been a change of plans. What are you doing?" he asked as she bent down and picked up the pair of red sandals that the young woman who she now assumed was Alessandra, had left next to the bar. She put them in her purse.

"I'll tell you all about it later," she said feeling his hand on her back, pushing her towards the front door.

"Kelly, hurry up," he said taking long strides towards their rental car.

"I am, Mike, but I can't walk as fast as you can. What's the rush? Why are we going to the B and B and then the sheriff's station?"

"My chief deputy, Brandon Wynn, called while you were in the restroom. Half of my staff is out sick, and he said the rest of them look like they will be by tomorrow. He said I need to get back as soon as possible." Just then Mike's phone rang, and he said, "Were you able to get us on a plane?" He listened to his secretary for a moment. "That's fine. Three hours from now will be perfect. We can make it. Tell Deputy Wynn I'm on my way and tell him to go home. He sounded horrible when I talked to him." Mike was quiet again and then said, "Yes, you go on home, too. I'll see you in a couple of days."

CHAPTER TWENTY-SEVEN

When Kelly and Mike got back to the B & B, Mike said, "Kelly, you go up and start packing. I'll settle our bill and be up in a few minutes."

"10-4," Kelly said and practically ran up the stairs two at a time. As soon as she entered the room, she began to throw things in their suitcases. Mike came up in a few minutes and double-checked that she hadn't missed anything in the closet or the bathroom. "Looks good, Kelly. Thanks." They hurried down the hall to the stairs and a few moments later were on their way to the sheriff's station.

"We just barely have enough time to stop at the sheriff's station on our way out of town, but I want to let him know why we're leaving," Mike said, hitting the gas pedal. "I feel like I'm letting him down, but unfortunately, as an elected official, I have an obligation to my constituents, and having a sheriff's station understaffed with less than the needed number of deputies on duty would really be a disaster. As it is, I hope I can make it back before everyone has gone home. I'll have to go into the station as soon as we get back to Cedar Bay."

"I understand. Your being there takes precedence. So your secretary had no problem changing our tickets?" Kelly asked.

"She said we had to pay a little bit more to change them, but it wasn't much, and really, there was no choice. Good, I see the sheriff's car is parked in the lot, so that probably means he's here."

They walked into the station and Mike said, "I'm Sheriff Reynolds. Would you please tell Sheriff Dawson I'm here? I have some things I need to run by him, and I have an airplane flight I need to catch in Sacramento, so I'm sort of in a hurry."

After the young officer at the desk had called the sheriff, he said, "Please go back to his office. He said you've been there before." Kelly and Mike opened the door and walked down the hall to Sheriff Dawson's office.

"Come in," Sheriff Dawson said in answer to Mike's knock. "Good to see you. How are you both doing today?"

"Been better, Sheriff. There's a flu bug going around back at my office, and half of my staff is out with it, and the other half is expected to come down with it momentarily. My chief deputy called and told me I really need to get back. I feel like we're abandoning you, but I don't have a choice. I'm sure you'd do the same thing under the same circumstances, but we have found out a few things." He turned to Kelly and said, "Why don't you start?"

Kelly told him about her conversation with the owner of The Shoe Salon and then removed a pair of small red sandals from her purse. "Sheriff, I have a feeling that the soleprint on these sandals will match the soleprints that were found on the stairs leading up to the top of the vat, and I think I know who they belong to and who the killer is."

"Kelly, you never told me that," Mike said with a look of surprise on his face.

"I never had a chance. We had to leave the Romano Winery Tasting Room in such a rush I didn't have time to tell you what I found out while I was in the restroom." She told both of them about the conversation she'd overheard when she was in the restroom as well as the conversation she'd overheard coming from Carlos

Romano's office.

Sheriff Dawson sat back in his chair and twirled a pencil between his fingers. "Kelly, I agree with you. I think you've discovered that Alessandra Romano murdered Angela Lucci, but it's an awful lot of circumstantial evidence. The soleprints on the red sandals, what you overheard, all of it points to her, but I don't think the District Attorney will consider it enough to bring charges."

"I might be able to help you there, Sheriff," Mike said. He turned to Kelly and said, "I haven't had a chance to tell you this either, but when I was on the golf course this morning I got a call from Jim Barstow, the manager of the Moretti Winery. He told me he'd gotten a call last night from Juan Sabbatini, the man who's in charge of his vineyards and the hiring of the help. He said one of his workers had called yesterday at the urging of his wife, because he'd seen a woman go into the vat barn about the time Angela was murdered.

"Jim asked if the man could identify the woman, either in person or from a photograph, and he said yes, because it was still light out. He was waiting for his wife to pick him up, and he didn't recognize the woman, so he watched her as she walked from her parked car down to the vat barn. He said what he thought was strange was she didn't walk in a straight line, but kind of tried to hide behind some of the grape vines. She'd crouch down behind one and then go from one to another. He said she reached down and petted a dog tied to a post just outside the vat barn door, and then she disappeared inside. He said his wife was late and he was still waiting for her a few minutes later when he heard the dog barking frantically. He said he saw the woman's face when she hurried up the lane to where her car was parked. She got in it and drove away real fast.

"Evidently the man was taking the next morning off to attend the funeral of a relative. His wife had heard about the murder and asked him when he returned if he'd seen anything. That was when he told her about seeing a strange woman enter the vat barn. She told the man he should call Juan, that maybe what he saw would be of help."

"Are you kidding? Sheriff Dawson said. "If he could identify the woman going in and out of the barn at the time of the murder, we'd have an eyeball witness, and that may be the tipping point for circumstantial evidence we already have."

"Knowing what we know now, I agree," Mike said. "I planned on going out to the winery this afternoon and talking to the man. Based on what Kelly told you, maybe you could get a picture of Alessandra and see if he can ID her."

"I'm sure I can get a picture one way or another. Excuse me, but my secretary never puts a call through when I have people in my office unless it's an emergency. I need to take this one." He listened for several minutes, hung up his phone, turned to Kelly and Mike and said, "I think you two solved the murder."

Sheriff Dawson abruptly stood up and grabbed his hat. "I need to leave. Here's what just happened. A 911 call just came in from the Romano Winery Tasting Room. It was from Carlos Romano. All the big-time wine growers have a panic button under their desk that's wired to 911. There have been a lot of robberies at the tasting rooms in town. After he pushed the button he called 911 and said his niece, Alessandra Romano, was having a mental breakdown, and he'd instructed his security guards to restrain her. He said to send an ambulance as well. He said she was screaming she'd killed Angela Lucci, and she was threatening to commit suicide. The Angela Lucci case may be over shortly. I'm on my way there now. I'll call you later on and let you know what happens. Thanks for everything," he said as he rushed out to his car and tore out of the parking lot, red lights blinking and siren screaming.

Kelly and Mike stared at each other for several moments in disbelief. Mike was the first to break the silence. "Well, we could have scripted a lot of outcomes to this whole thing, but this was one I never saw coming. Let's go. We really do need to hurry. Don't forget, we've got to turn in our rental car and then try and catch our flight. It's going to be a close call."

EPILOGUE

The following day an exhausted Mike called Kelly and said, "Just call me General Custer, because I think I'm the last man standing. Pray nothing major happens in the county that needs the attention of the sheriff's department. I should have a few people back tomorrow. This had to be about the most contagious flu that's ever been around. Anyway, I got a call from Sheriff Dawson, and I wanted to fill you in on what's happened."

"I'm all ears. I don't think I've thought of anything else since we left his office yesterday. Well, I take that back. When we were running through the Sacramento airport trying to catch our flight, I wasn't thinking of it. In fact, we were in such a hurry, I didn't even have time to wonder why the airport authorities decided to hang a fifty-foot-tall modern art rendition of a rabbit from the ceiling in the terminal next to the escalators. Talk about some weird versions of public art. I think the dumb rabbit wins."

"Yeah, making it onto our plane was an adventure." Mike began to laugh. "Being the last people to get on a plane has never been the cause of a lowered blood pressure, and mine sure wasn't very low by the time we got seated. You better sit down. This is going to take a few minutes."

"Okay, I have my glass of iced tea. I put Lady, Rebel, and Skyy out, and you have my undivided attention. Shoot."

"Alessandra Romano continued to scream that she killed Angela Lucci, because she loved Matteo. She even blurted out how she crept up the stairs of the vat, grabbed Angela from behind, held her face over the carbon dioxide gas coming from the vat until she passed out, and then pushed her into the vat. The paramedics finally gave her a strong sedative to calm her down. Evidently, they were afraid she was going to break through her restraints. That's one thing. Sheriff Dawson had a long talk with Carlos Romano, who is grieving not only over his niece's mental breakdown, but also about the fact that he blames himself for what happened. He said if he hadn't made a casual offhand comment about Angela falling into the vat, it never would have happened."

"I doubt that. He might have planted the seeds, but it sounds like she was pretty unstable to start with."

"You're right. He told the sheriff that the reason the family had sent her to Carlos in the first place was because of her instability. They were hoping that a new environment and the psychiatrist she was seeing would help her. It didn't."

"What about the sandals and the vineyard worker?" Kelly asked.

"The soles of the red sandals you gave to the sheriff matched the soleprints that were found on the stairs. The sheriff took a picture of Alessandra and had one of his deputies, who was fluent in Spanish, drive out to the vineyard and meet with Juan and the worker. The worker identified the woman in the picture as being the same woman he had seen go in and out of the vat barn."

"Mike, if they just showed him one picture, wouldn't he naturally identify her as being the one he'd seen?"

"Yes, if they had done that, he probably would have, but they wanted to cross all their t's and dot their i's, although unless Alessandra's condition changes radically, she'll probably never be able to stand trial but instead will wind up in a mental institution. Anyway, the worker was shown five photographs of women, one of whom was Caitlin, the intern. He absolutely confirmed that Alessandra was the one he'd seen."

"Well, that pretty much sums it up, doesn't it?"

"Yes, except for one thing which I think you'll find quite interesting. As we found out, there can't be any down time at a vineyard. In other words, there must be a winemaker and guess who Carlos Romano hired?"

"I haven't a clue, since I don't know any other winemakers in the valley or really, anywhere else, for that matter."

"Well, I've got news for you. You've met her."

"Seriously? It can't have been the woman who owns the shoe shop, and I think the only other woman I talked to for any length of time was Josie. Was it her? Although I don't see her leaving the Morettis and going over to the Romano Winery."

"You're getting warmer. Remember the young woman, Caitlin Sanders, who was so anxious to become a winemaker that she'd even called *Signor* Moretti when she found out that Angela was dead? Well, she called Carlos Romano, and the timing must have been right. He called the university and talked to the dean of the department who he knows well. I guess all the winemakers know him. Anyway, he said Caitlin was a brilliant young woman and would probably make an excellent winemaker. Kind of a full circle, huh?"

There was dead silence on Kelly's end of the line. It was so long Mike finally said, "Kelly are you there?"

"I'm here Mike, but I'm in shock. Somehow it doesn't seem right that she got that job. I suppose it will be interesting to see what happens. An even fuller circle would be if she and Matteo ended up together. However, as focused on wine as I understand Caitlin is, I don't think that's a likely possibility."

"From the tone of your voice, I'm getting the impression you hope that will never happen."

"I do. I think Matteo deserves more."

"Only because he reminds you of your son. Speaking of children, when I get home I want to call Julia and see how Ella's doing. I also want to start making plans for our trip to Disneyland. I can't decide whether we should stay in that hotel that has a tram that goes directly to the park or at some beach hotel, so the girls can play in the ocean. What do you think?"

"I think we need to have a long talk. Love you, Sheriff, I mean General Custer."

"Love you, too."

RECIPES

MEXICAN SALAD WITH RASPBERRY CHIPOTLE DRESSING

Ingredients:
1 skinless boneless chicken breast
1 tsp. olive oil + ¼ cup olive oil
½ tsp. coriander
½ tsp. cumin
½ tsp. salt
¼ tsp. pepper
1 head Romaine lettuce, roughly chopped
2 Roma tomatoes, diced
¼ cup canned corn
1 small red onion, diced
4 small corn tortillas, cut into strips ½ inch wide, 3 inches long (If you prefer, you can use packaged strips.)
4 tbsp. cilantro, chopped
1 ½ cups Raspberry Chipotle sauce (The one I use is Fischer Wieser and comes in a plastic bottle. It's available online, but I get it at Costco. I'm sure you can find something similar.)

Directions:
Preheat oven to 400 degrees if you're going to make your own tortilla strips.) Using a sharp fillet knife, butterfly the chicken breast into 2 separate pieces. Cut each of the them into thin pieces, so you

have 8 to 10 pieces ½ inch wide by 3 inches in length. (Don't worry, this isn't about precision. Irregular pieces or nuggets work fine). Sprinkle cumin, coriander, salt, and pepper on both sides of the chicken pieces. Coat a frying pan with 1 tsp. olive oil and fry the chicken pieces over medium heat for 3 minutes on each side. Remove them from the pan and cut them into bite size pieces.

Brush the tortilla strips with olive oil, place on a cookie sheet, and bake for 10 minutes or until crisp. Remove from the oven and set aside. Whisk the Raspberry Chipotle sauce and ¼ cup olive oil together to make the dressing.

Combine all of the ingredients together in a bowl with the exception of the dressing and gently toss. Plate the salad and drizzle the dressing over the top. Enjoy!

GOLD STAR MOTHER'S DAY DESSERT

Ingredients:
4 oz. mascarpone cheese, softened to room temperature
4 oz. whipped topping, such as Cool Whip (If you're so inclined, you can whip your own.)
¼ cup white chocolate chips (I like to use the best I can find, but it's not necessary. Any brand will do.)
2 dozen fresh strawberries, hulled and diced (Reserve 4 strawberries for garnish. If you prefer, you can use raspberries.)
1 cup fresh blueberries
4 parfait glasses or other type of clear glass containers

Directions:
Microwave the chocolate chips for about 15 seconds or so. Stir until melted and add the mascarpone cheese. Stir until smooth and add the whipped topping. Stir gently to combine.

Assembly:
Divide the ingredients equally by adding a spoonful or two of the diced strawberries into the parfait glasses. Top with a dollop of the

cream mixture. Add a layer of blueberries and another layer of cream. Continue layering until everything has been used. Depending on the size of the glasses, you may have some leftover, so make extras! Garnish with a strawberry. These can be made several hours in advance. Refrigerate. Serve and enjoy!

MUFFIN MEAT LOAVES

Ingredients:
1 ½ lb. lean ground beef
1 ½ cups shredded zucchini
1 tsp. garlic powder
½ tsp. dried Italian seasoning
½ tsp. salt
¼ tsp. freshly ground pepper
½ cup bread crumbs (You can use fresh, but I'm a fan of Panko crumbs.)
¼ cup water
¼ cup barbecue sauce (Everyone has their favorite brand. Mine is Sweet Baby Ray's.)
Non-stick cooking spray

Directions:
Preheat oven to 350 degrees. Lightly spray the cup in a 12-cup muffin tin. In a large bowl thoroughly combine all the ingredients but the barbecue sauce.

Place about 1/3 cup of the mixture into each of 12 medium muffin cups. Press down lightly. Spread a little barbecue sauce on top of each one. Bake about 25 minutes, or until no longer pink. Serve and enjoy!

NOTE: I was worried I'd get an excessive amount of grease in the muffin cups, since I use pork when I make meat loaf. With the lean beef, that's not a problem, and they come out of the tins quite easily. You could also use mini-muffin tins to make appetizers, just adjust your cooking time.

PAPPARDELLE CARBONARA

Ingredients:
12 oz. pappardelle pasta
8 slices prosciutto, thinly sliced (That's probably two packages.)
1 tbs. olive oil
3 eggs (I like jumbo.)
¾ cup cream
½ cup finely grated Parmesan cheese
¼ cup coarsely chopped fresh basil

Directions:
Cook pasta according to directions in a large pot of boiling water (put enough salt in it so it tastes like the ocean) until tender. Drain and reserve ½ cup liquid. Return the pasta to the pan over low heat.

While the pasta is cooking, cook the prosciutto in olive oil in large frying pan until crisp. Combine eggs, cream, and cheese in a mixing bowl. Add the mixture, the reserved cooking liquid, half the parsley, and half the prosciutto to the pasta, lightly tossing.

Serve pasta topped with remaining prosciutto and parsley. Enjoy!

TOMATO TAPAS

Ingredients:
2 large tomatoes
1 baguette
8 garlic cloves, papery coating removed, and finely chopped
¼ cup extra virgin olive oil
¼ cup balsamic vinegar
Salt and pepper to taste
8 fresh basil leaves, rolled together and finely chopped

Directions:
Slice the tomatoes into rounds, discarding the ends. Slice the baguette lengthwise and then slice each half into four pieces. Put 1/8

of the garlic on each piece and top with ½ tbsp. olive oil. Distribute the tomato slices evenly over the pieces and top with ½ tbsp. balsamic vinegar. Salt and pepper to taste. Scatter the basil over all. Serve and enjoy!

NOTE: I have used several kinds of baguettes and all work fine. I have also used bagels. What doesn't work is bread. It's too soft, and the whole thing becomes mushy and unappetizing. Matter of fact, we have fresh tomatoes most of the year, and it's my go-to breakfast!

Paperbacks & Ebooks for FREE

Go to www.dianneharman.com/freepaperback.html and get your FREE copies of Dianne's books and favorite recipes immediately by signing up for her newsletter.

Once you've signed up for her newsletter you're eligible to win three paperbacks. One lucky winner is picked every week. Hurry before the offer ends!

ABOUT THE AUTHOR

Dianne lives in Huntington Beach, California, with her husband, Tom, a former California State Senator, and her boxer dog, Kelly. Her passions are cooking, reading, and dogs, so whenever she has a little free time, you can either find her in the kitchen, playing with Kelly in the back yard, or curled up with the latest book she's reading.

Her award winning books include:

Cedar Bay Cozy Mystery Series
Kelly's Koffee Shop, Murder at Jade Cove, White Cloud Retreat, Marriage and Murder, Murder in the Pearl District, Murder in Calico Gold, Murder at the Cooking School, Murder in Cuba, Trouble at the Kennel, Murder on the East Coast, Trouble at the Animal Shelter, Murder & The Movie Star, Murdered by Wine

Liz Lucas Cozy Mystery Series
Murder in Cottage #6, Murder & Brandy Boy, The Death Card, Murder at The Bed & Breakfast, The Blue Butterfly, Murder at the Big T Lodge, Murder in Calistoga

High Desert Cozy Mystery Series
Murder & The Monkey Band, Murder & The Secret Cave, Murdered by Country Music, Murder at the Polo Club, Murdered by Plastic Surgery

Midwest Cozy Mystery Series
Murdered by Words, Murder at the Clinic

Jack Trout Cozy Mystery Series
Murdered in Argentina

Northwest Cozy Mystery Series
Murder on Bainbridge Island, Murder in Whistler, Murder in Seattle

Coyote Series
Blue Coyote Motel, Coyote in Provence, Cornered Coyote

Midlife Journey Series
Alexis

Newsletter

If you would like to be notified of her latest releases please go to www.dianneharman.com and sign up for her newsletter.

Website: www.dianneharman.com,
Blog: www.dianneharman.com/blog
Email: dianne@dianneharman.com

Made in the USA
Columbia, SC
25 September 2017